D

Pan

2/2/2006

Rewind

Paul Manship

PONT

*For three special girls
Olivia, Rosie and Alice*

First Impression – 2006

ISBN 1 84323 591 9

© Paul Manship, 2006

Paul Manship has asserted his right under the
Copyright, Designs and Patents Act, 1988,
to be identified as Author of this Work.

All rights reserved. No part of this book may be
reproduced, stored in a retrieval system, or transmitted
in any form or by any means, electronic, electrostatic,
magnetic tape, mechanical, photocopying, recording or
otherwise without permission in writing from the
publishers, Pont Books, Gomer Press, Llandysul,
Ceredigion.

This book is published with the financial support of the
Welsh Books Council.

*Printed in Wales at
Gomer Press, Llandysul, Ceredigion SA44 4JL*

Chapter 1

Perfect Start

'Arrtttiieeeeee!!! Wake up!!! You're going to be late!!!'

Artie. That's me. And the ear-splitting screech belongs to my mum.

And it's no surprise that I'm going to be late. I'm *always* late. If she would only wake me up at eight o'clock, like any normal mother, then I wouldn't be. Half past eight is no good to me! I live about a hundred and fifty miles away from the school – well, at least *one* mile, anyway.

I'm in Year Six at Our Lady of the Blessed Angels Junior School, Bettws, Newport, South Wales, Europe, the Northern Hemisphere, the Earth, the Solar System, the Milky Way.

Many of the residents of Bettws think the name of my school is a joke, probably because there aren't actually many 'angels' on the register. Last term alone, three pupils were excluded, and one lucky individual – Damien Harris – was chucked out altogether. Damien is probably lying in bed at this very moment, planning which games to play on his play-station.

I can feel a bad day coming on. Another one.

I've definitely had more than my share of bad days over the last eleven years! Starting with the day I was born, when my parents hit on the bright idea of calling me Artie, or Art for short (after my grandfather Arthur). *Art*, for goodness sake! I sound like a subject you learn in school. They might as well have called me Geography or Science! And you can guess the fun the other kids have finding rhymes for my name. Artie?

As I struggle to force my arm through my inside-out shirt sleeve, another ear-splitting screech shakes my bedroom walls: 'Nooooooooooooooooooooooooooo!'

My mum is going through the daily ritual of dressing my sister Sali. It's very difficult to put clothes on a three-year-old who refuses to wear anything with buttons. A second shriek, even louder than the first, erupts from Sali's lungs: 'NOOOOOOOOOOOOOOO!'

So much sound from such a little person!

I know where *I'd* like to put the buttons!

I block out the noise, throw my clothes on, pelt down the stairs, grab a biscuit and head out the back door.

My mum's voice follows after me: 'Don't forget to clean your teeth!'

If she's that concerned about my dental health, why doesn't she wake me up at a civilized time?

It usually takes me about twenty minutes to get to school. I live right on the other side of the estate from Our Lady's. It's my privilege to live further away from school than any other pupil! Isn't life great? My feet hardly touch the ground as I fly down Monnow Way, the road that runs right round the Bettws estate.

It's just gone nine o'clock as I sneak, burglar-like, past the headmaster's window and then stroll across the empty hall, straining with every bone in my body not to look suspicious.

Our classroom door stands open, as it always does. Some of my classmates notice me but Mr Batty doesn't. It's Monday morning and he's doing battle with the dinner register while the class is engaged in handwriting practice. It's dead quiet.

Mr Batty has been sucked into Dinner Register World! I bet he wouldn't even notice if my classmates all came and joined me at the door!

I can just imagine Mr Batty glancing up and finding himself, literally, in a class of his own! Off he'd go, scuttling round the school, searching for his missing pupils. And then he'd bump into Mr Griffiths, our head, and he'd have to confess that he'd – um – misplaced his class.

'You've *what*!!??'

'I seem to have lost some . . . children, Mr Griffiths.'

'Children? How many children exactly?'

'Uh – all of them.'

'All of them!!??'

It would make the front page of the South Wales Argus: TEACHER LOSES CLASS!

A snigger escapes from my lips.

Mr Batty looks up.

'Ah! Mr King! How nice of you to join us!' he says welcomingly. 'Prynhawn da!'

Good afternoon? Now I *know* I'm in trouble! 'Good afternoon – I mean good morning, sir.'

Mr Batty stands up and heads towards me. He is wearing an enormous grin, but I'm not fooled. Great White Sharks have enormous grins too!

He wraps his arm around my shoulder and leads

me to the front of the class, just where I *don't* want to be.

'Look everyone,' he announces, 'it's Mr King! He has decided to honour us with his regal presence. Let's all say "good morning", shall we?'

I can practically smell the sarcasm seeping from Mr Batty. Do teachers get special lessons at training college or something?

'*BORE DA, ARTIE!*' my classmates sing out in chorus.

'Children,' Mr Batty declares (he's in lecture mode now), 'this young man clearly thinks it's clever to wander in at whatever time he chooses. He doesn't think school is important; he doesn't think end-of-year tests are important; he obviously doesn't think his *future* is important.'

'Sir! Sir!' pipes up Rhys Williams, as ever picking the wrong moment. 'That's ten pence you owe us!'

Over the last few weeks, in an attempt to be cool – unsuccessful, I might add – Mr Batty has come up with this idea whereby every time he mentions the word 'tests', he has to put ten pence in a jam-jar. Already there must be over five pounds in there! He can't stop talking about tests! He *lives* and *breathes* them! I bet he has *dreams* about tests!

'Not now, Rhys Williams!'

Sir is obviously not in a generous mood.

I try in vain to slip free from his grasp but he has a grip stronger than a demented koala.

'Well, children,' he drones on (and on and on . . .), 'I'd like you to be aware that King here is *not* going to get away with his persistent lack of punctuality. Our illustrious headmaster has decided that, from now on, every time children wander in late, they will be spending morning break outside the office. And, if this lateness continues, King will not be joining the rest of us on our end-of-term trip to Oakwood Theme Park. I hope I'm making myself clear!'

Mr Batty puts his mouth right up against my ear, so close to me that I can smell the kippers he must have had for breakfast. 'Am I making myself clear?'

'Yes, sir,' I mutter, staring down at my trainers. They have seen better days – a lot like Mr Batty, really.

I walk to the back of the class and slump into my chair.

'Sit up straight, boy!' comes the immediate shout.

Well, this is going well, I think to myself. And it's not even half past nine yet! I decide to keep my head down and try and stay out of trouble for the rest of the day . . .

I manage to last until 10.25, when I make the unfortunate error of sitting next to the wrong person during assembly.

We are about halfway through the school prayer when Callum Young, sitting to my immediate left, decides to roll up his sleeve and create a huge raspberry noise by blowing as hard as he can on his arm.

The prayer comes to a sudden halt.

All eyes point to where the sound came from.

Glancing to my left, I can see that Callum must have recently had acting lessons – he looks the picture of innocence! I, on the other hand, am as red as the rows of jerseys sitting in front of and behind me.

'King,' says Mr Griffiths calmly. 'Leave us.' He never shouts in front of a crowd. He reserves his shouting for the office.

'But, sir,' I protest, 'it wasn't me.'

'Of course it was you,' he says. 'I don't have to be Sherlock Holmes to solve this case, you know. Sudden loud noise. Red-faced child. Case solved.'

Old Griffiths can be quite funny when he wants to be. The rest of the school seems to find it funny anyway.

I can't believe the injustice of it. This is bad luck, even by my standards!

'But, sir,' I defend myself, 'I'm telling you . . .'

'You are not telling me *anything*, boy! Go and wait for me outside my office – right now!'

I stand up, my fists clenched and my eyes watering. Two hundred pairs of eyes are fixed on me. I can't ever remember feeling so angry before. I am a volcano and can't control the eruption that follows.

'I'M SICK OF THIS STUPID PLACE!' I bellow, and then stomp out of the hall, kicking some of the PE apparatus along the way.

This is not helping my case at all!

I locate the chair outside the office and slam myself down in it, nearly putting a hole in the wall and causing the secretary to shout a warning. 'Hey!'

This chair is quite familiar to me. I have sat in it many times. They ought to put my name on it!

Because I'm such a frequent occupant, I've taught myself a little trick to help the time pass more quickly. I close my eyes and picture myself in a time-machine. I choose a date from the past, press some buttons and go whizzing and swirling through time and space. Since being in Year Six, I've travelled to Roman times, Tudor times, Victorian times and the Second World War – and all of them are better than the present day!

I love history and find it easy to imagine what life was like during different periods. Today I decide to visit the Dark Ages and do battle with some Picts – and they all look like Callum Young . . .

My foot is being tapped. By someone else's.

It's Mr Griffiths.

That was quick! Assembly over already! And my life probably, too!

'Right. You,' he points, 'in there!'

He follows me in and closes the door.

I hate this office. It's cramped, there's no air, and it smells! I can't imagine anything worse than spending the day in here! I almost feel sorry for Mr Griffiths.

Almost.

He sits down on the corner of his desk. Why he does this, when he has a perfectly good chair to sit on, I have no idea.

The lecture begins.

'I don't know what's wrong with you, King. You used to be such a nice lad. Mrs Lewis always said what a good boy you were – a credit to the school. Well, you're not a credit to anybody at the moment. We've all pretty much had enough of your silly behaviour and attitude, I don't mind telling you. Heaven help you in the High School, that's all I can say – and Heaven help the High School too!'

He stops talking. Everything goes quiet. I'm not sure if I'm supposed to say something.

He lets out a sigh and then continues. 'I'll be speaking to your mother in a moment and I'll be informing her that, as from today, Mr Batty will be keeping a record of your behaviour, which will be sent home with you at the end of each afternoon. If there is no noticeable improvement in the next few weeks, not only can you wave goodbye to the Oakwood trip, but you'll also be looking forward to spending lunchtimes at home. I'm sure that'll make your mum very happy.'

More sarcasm.

There doesn't seem to be much point in protesting my innocence. It's a done deal. Signed. Sealed. Delivered.

'Now get out of my sight!'

Apparently the meeting is over.

I'd been expecting lines or a missed break. Boy, did I underestimate the size of my problems!

I make my way outside. Playtime is pretty much over. Some of the kids are in the yard but most of them are on the field. The sun is out, but it doesn't seem to be shining on me at the moment.

I decide to go and find Gwyneth. She's in my reading group. Rhys Williams says she wants to go out with me. I spot her standing under the goalposts. She has this flame of red hair that makes her stand out in a crowd. She's doing handstands with her mates, Rachel and Clare.

'Well, what a great day *I'm* having!' I comment.

'Did somebody say something?' says Clare. She's

Gwyneth's best friend and urgently needs a personality makeover.

'I don't think so,' chips in Rachel. *She* could do with some treatment too! 'It must have been the wind.'

'What's up, Gwyneth!' I enquire, ignoring her two bodyguards.

'Did you hear that?' Clare cups her hand to her ear.

'Hear what?' Rachel shrugs.

'I could have sworn I heard a little voice.'

I attempt to move around them to speak to Gwyneth face-to-face, but her bodyguards move with me. From a distance, we must look like a troupe of folk-dancers.

As we all twirl around, Clare yells in my face, 'Can't you see she doesn't want to talk to you!'

Then Rachel joins in. 'She doesn't want to be seen with a crude little boy like you. Let's face it, King, you're just not cool.'

I can't be bothered with this. I decide to go and sit in the shade. We're quite lucky in our school – we've got this huge field, and its got these droopy looking trees around part of it, so you can sit under them and cool off if you get too hot.

I slump down on the grass under my favourite tree, as far away from other human beings as possible.

So . . . I'm not cool. They're probably right about that. I certainly don't feel cool.

I close my eyes and spend some quality-time chopping the heads off more Picts, all of them clones of Callum Young.

Chapter 2

Smashing Time

Eleven o'clock finds me back in the classroom, quiet and subdued.

'And now,' begins Mr Batty, 'a spot of science revision. Only three weeks to go to our end-of-year tests.'

'Ten pence, sir!' pipes up Rhys Williams, right on cue.

'Thank you, Rhys. What would I do without you?'

We now have £5.30 in the cookie-jar.

'Sir! Sir!'

'Yes, Rhys.'

'You haven't collected our homework in yet.'

Homework? I don't remember being given any homework . . .

'Oh yes,' says Mr Batty, holding his finger in the air, 'I nearly forgot. Thank you, Rhys.'

Yes. Thank you, Rhys. Thank you *so* much. Next time I visit the Dark Ages, Rhys Williams is going to be right there, losing his head alongside Callum Young.

Twenty five pairs of hands are now rummaging through their desk-trays.

I seriously do *not* remember being given any homework.

Mr Batty is already circulating, collecting in the offerings. It's not long before he's standing in front of me with his hand open.

'Well?' he says. He's enjoying this. It must be obvious I haven't got it.

'I haven't got it, sir,' I admit. May as well come clean. I can't magic it out of thin air, can I?

'Well, well! What a surprise, everyone!' (He's got his sarcasm hat on again!) 'King hasn't got his homework.' He bends towards me, 'And may one be allowed to enquire where it is?'

'I haven't done it, sir. I don't think I was in when you gave it out, sir.' I tend to say 'sir' a lot when I'm on the defensive.

'Don't give me that. This homework was set last Monday. I reminded people about it at least three times last week. You've had ample time and opportunity to do it, wouldn't you agree?'

How can I not agree? He has me on the ropes.

Mr Batty now addresses the rest of the class. '6B, let's have a show of hands. Hands up if you think it's fair that *you* all have to do homework but King here doesn't.'

Only one hand in the air. Danny Morgan's. He obviously hasn't understood the question.

Mr Batty looks at him like he's an alien from another universe. 'Put your hand down, Danny. Right. I'm not wasting any more of the class's time on you, King. I'll expect your homework tomorrow morning. Is that clear?'

Crystal.

I don't even know what the homework is. Perhaps I won't be very well tomorrow. My throat feels a bit sore.

Fortunately I manage to survive the rest of the lesson without being told off or humiliated. I even know a few of the answers to Mr Batty's questions. Of course, I don't get to share them with the rest of the class because he never picks me, even though my arm is long and I wave it about quite a lot.

At lunchtime, I return to my spot in the shade and take up where I left off, hacking pieces from a never-ending horde of Callum/Rhys look-alikes.

A magpie comes and sits next to me for a bit. Just the *one* magpie, as you'd expect – one for sorrow, two for joy and all that . . .

I feel a tap on my shoulder and swivel around. It's Gavin Price, a snotty little kid from Year Three.

'Oy, you,' he says, wiping his nose along his sleeve (these younger kids have no respect), 'Mrs Moss wants to see you.'

Mrs Moss is queen of the dinner ladies. This doesn't sound at all good. It's highly unlikely that I'm about to receive a certificate or sticker. I'm trying to remember what I've done wrong.

'She wants you *now*,' green-sleeved Gavin persists.

'All right! Hold your horses.'

I start making my way across the field towards the area outside 4L, where Mrs Moss spends her lunchtimes with a daily assortment of casualties and hangers-on.

As I arrive, I notice a Year Four boy sitting on a chair next to her with his head between his legs.

Mrs Moss doesn't give me chance before she begins her assault. 'Right, what have you got to say for yourself?'

I shrug. Not the best tactic with grown-ups, I ought to know by now.

'Don't act the innocent with me, young man!' she scolds. 'Craig here says that you kicked him.'

'I never, miss.'

I hadn't. *Really*, I hadn't.

I could tell by the look in her eyes that I wasn't going to get a fair hearing.

Not today.

'Why would Craig say you did if you didn't?'

Search me! He's blind? He's stupid? He's got me mixed up with someone else? Who knows?

'Don't know, miss,' is all I can come up with.

'No, of course you don't,' she says. 'You don't seem to know much at *all*, do you. Like, for example, the school rules! *Keep hands, feet and objects to yourself.* You don't seem to be familiar with that one.'

Actually, she is wrong. I am very familiar with the rules. I have them quoted to me on a regular basis.

'Right,' Mrs Moss points at me, 'your name is going in my book.'

Wonderful. Thanks, Mrs Moss. Just what I need.

I am to find out later that it is Ryan Snelling who has kicked Craig. Apparently Craig called him Smelling instead of Snelling and he got a bit upset about it. Some people say Ryan Snelling looks like me, but I can't see it myself. Obviously, Craig thinks so. The only thing we've got in common is ging . . . auburn hair.

Anyway, where's justice when you need it? I'm in the book and that's that!

The afternoon plods along and three o'clock finds my classmates and me on the field for Games. Mr Taylor is holding trials for the school baseball squad. Yes, baseball! Not the American version, though. This is the Welsh version, as played in Newport and Cardiff. The ball is white and hard as I know from experience! The bat is similar to a cricket bat but the batter stands differently and the bowler bowls underarm.

I love the game. Probably because I'm quite good at it. Actually, to tell the truth, I'm *very* good at it. I'm the strongest batsman in the school, even if I say so myself. I can't kick a football to save my life, but once I'm standing at those pegs with a bat in my hand, I feel invincible.

I was in the squad last year, even though I was only in Year Five, so it's a dead cert that I'll keep my place this year!

Mr Taylor sits us down and picks two teams. I am chosen as one of the captains. Things are looking promising.

Twenty minutes into the game and my side is winning by a mile. I've already hit three home-runs, one of which nearly goes through the windscreen of Mr Batty's Volvo!

It's my turn again. I'm at the pegs, trusty bat in

hand. I look around at all the spaces the fielders have left wide open. Nicky Lingard bowls to me, just where I want it. The ball connects beautifully with my bat and I send it out between second and third bases. Unbelievably, Lewis Roberts manages to stop it with his outstretched hand. I've already touched first base and I'm on my way to second. Someone behind me shouts: 'Move it!!' I put on a spurt and arrive at second-base a split-second before the ball does. Phew!

But then Mr Taylor points at me and yells: 'Outtttt!'

'No way!' I hear myself gasp.

'Yes, way,' smiles Mr Taylor. 'You were out, Artie. Only *just*. But you were definitely out.'

I am not leaving the field. There is no way that I could possibly have been out. Mr Taylor needs to get his eyes tested.

'Move, King!' he roars. 'You're holding everybody up!'

I stay rooted to the spot for a few more seconds then storm off the pitch, swearing under my breath as I go.

'Come here, Artie!' Mr Taylor beckons as I walk past him. He can't have heard me swear, can he? I ignore him and keep right on walking.

'OK then, don't come here. Just keep right on walking, and don't bother turning around until you get to Mr Griffiths's office. Do not pass Go. Do not collect £200.'

Under normal circumstances, I like Mr Taylor. But these are not normal circumstances.

And there's more to come!

'By the way,' he continues to bellow after me, 'don't

bother coming to training next week because you're DROPPED!'

This is the last thing I need to hear. The word 'dropped' causes my heart to sink. I stand still, head bowed. Of course, I *could* go and apologise. But my stubbornness and pride won't let me.

I report to Mr Griffiths's office for the second time in one day (not unusual for me, I have to say – my record is four). By the time he's finished with me, and explained that my mother hasn't been answering her phone today (thank goodness), I'm ten minutes later than everyone else leaving school.

Today has been right up there in the top-ten of the all-time worst days I have ever spent in Our Lady's.

Carrying the weight of the world on my shoulders, I stagger up the five flights of steps that lead to the school gate and the world at large.

As I step through the gates, I nearly trip over Jordan Bates and his two cronies. For some reason, they are crouched down behind the hedge. All three of them left Our Lady's last year and – let's put it this way – they haven't been greatly missed, Jordan in particular! I'm an angel in comparison, I swear.

'Well, well, well, look who it isn't!' says Jordan, kicking a hole in the hedge. 'It's Art-Attack! You're just in time. We could do with a bit of help.'

'Oh.'

This is *not* good.

'Yeah. As a matter of fact, we could. You see, we've

decided that we'd like to show Mr Griffiths how much we appreciate his school.'

My face must be a picture of confusion. 'That's nice,' I manage to say. I hope they don't spot the sarcasm. I'm starting to sound like Mr Batty.

'Yeah, we thought so too.'

'Yeah,' agree Wayne and Dean.

Wayne and Dean are not big talkers. I think they find it hard to string sentences together. Jordan definitely has the lion's share of the brains in their outfit – about ninety-nine per cent, I would estimate.

'We want to show the school,' Jordan continues, 'exactly what we think of it. We want to show Mr Griffiths that we think he is . . . uhhh . . . smashing . . . yeah, that's right . . . smashing.'

'Yeah, smashing.'

Is there an echo around here?

'Of course, we *could* send a card to the school, saying, *We think you're smashing!* but that would be a bit boring, wouldn't it?'

'Yeah, boring.'

Yet more echoes!

'So, what we're going to do is give our message more of a visual impact.'

Did I mention that Jordan is quite clever?

Wayne and Dean get straight to the point. 'We're gonna smash some windows.'

'What d'ya think?' Jordan asks me.

'Great idea,' I comment. The mood I'm in, I wouldn't care if the three of them climbed into a bull-dozer and demolished the whole school.

'We think so too,' Jordan grins. '*My* brainwave, of course.'

Obviously! That goes without saying. This plan is *far* too subtle for the other two!

'Have fun then,' I tell them and try to step past, but Jordan's leg is suddenly in my way.

'Hang on, mate,' he says, putting his leg down and his arm around my shoulder. 'We said we needed some help.'

Uh-oh. Here it comes.

Jordan walks me up and down the path. 'You're so lucky!' he exclaims. (He doesn't know the half of it!) 'You see, about two minutes ago, we decided that the next person to walk through these gates would be the one to help us. At first, we thought that maybe everybody had gone home. But then you walked out, the answer to our prayers.'

I wish someone would answer *my* prayers!

'So,' says Jordan, punching me on the arm. 'What d'ya say?'

I'm in enough trouble as it is. The last thing I need is to put a hole through a school window. 'Sorry,' I say, 'I'd like to help you, but I've gotta go. I'm late already.'

Jordan has a quizzical look on his face. He steps in close and squeezes my cheek 'playfully'. 'Will Mommy be worried if Artie-Fartie is a teensy-weensy bit late?' he mocks.

The other two are smirking at each other.

The pressure is on.

'What's the matter? Cat got your tongue?'

Jordan crouches down, and scoops up a large stone from under the hedge. He grabs my right hand and slaps the stone into my palm. 'Here's the rock,' he declares, 'and there's the window.' He is pointing at Mr Griffiths's room. 'I've seen you throw a baseball, King. You can't miss from here! Don't worry, nobody's watching!'

I glance around. He's right. No witnesses. No CCTV cameras.

However, what I *can* see is Mr Griffiths's back. He's drinking a cup of his herbal tea and working on his lap-top. The stone I'm holding is capable of doing a lot of damage – to the window *and* Mr Griffiths!

I step forward, turn the stone over in my hand a few times, take one last look behind me and then launch it with as much force as I can – at the ground. Unfortunately, at the last moment, Wayne decides to move . . . and takes the full impact of my guided missile . . . on his left foot.

I'm outta there.

Chapter 3

A Walk in the Park

I have no intention of stopping to administer first-aid to Wayne's foot!

I am out of there like a shot from a starting pistol! I rocket around the corner into Monnow Way, nearly separating a baby from its pram. I sprint for about three or four blocks. It's amazing the effect that fear has on my pace – an Olympic runner would have trouble catching me at this rate!

I decide to take a shortcut through the park but soon regret it. As I cut through the play-area, my co-ordination deserts me for a split-second and I find myself in a wrestling match with the swings, a match which I manage to lose!

Red-faced and watery-eyed, I pick myself up, brush myself down and continue on my way, limping past the park's solitary bench, which is currently occupied by an old man who appears to be asleep.

I make my way past him (he's dressed very smartly for this neighbourhood) and head for the gates at the other end of the park, but just as I reach them, my pathway is blocked – by Jordan Bates and the uninjured half of the twins! How could they have got here so fast, unless they'd run through people's gardens?

They stand there, arms folded, like two night-club bouncers. There is no point in trying to run *through* them. Dean looks like he's been doing weight-training since about the age of four and Jordan's just naturally hard! Everyone that I know is afraid of him.

I do an instant one hundred and eighty degree turn and head back past the bench. The old man looks very serene sitting there, like someone who has found inner peace. I could do with some inner peace right now!

As I negotiate the swings (more successfully this time), a figure emerges from behind the slide – a hobbling figure! Unbelievably, it's Wayne, looking none-too-happy. He moves towards me like some ancient mummy, dragging his foot behind him.

'You're dead, King,' he says. This is the most I've ever heard him say on his own.

I back away and turn around but freeze again. The other two are heading in my direction.

Both my exits are blocked!

The Oakwood trip looks out-of-the-question now. I'll probably be spending the next two months in hospital!

The old man begins to stir. He opens his eyes, stretches and yawns. I definitely haven't seen him round here before.

Now, before you say anything, I've had all the 'Stranger Danger' talks in school, so I know what's what, but right now, this old man is my only hope. So I go and sit next to him on the bench. He moves up to give me more room.

He is wearing a very smart pin-striped suit with a

blue silk tie and matching handkerchief. His hands are resting on the gold tip of this very impressive-looking walking-stick. He is wearing an earring! I have never seen a man his age wearing an earring before! It makes him look a bit like a pirate. A retired pirate!

His face looks rosy, as if he's spent most of his life outdoors. He has a white moustache that curls up on the ends and a trim little goatee beard. His head looks as if it's recently been shaved with one of those machines that barbers and sheep-shearers use. He looks completely out of place!

He squints at me. 'Hello there, young fella,' he yawns. He doesn't seem at all surprised that I'm sitting next to him.

Suddenly a shadow looms. Jordan and his buddies are standing directly in front of us. Now would be an ideal opportunity to make a break for it, but somehow I feel safer sitting here on the bench.

'Y'know, that wasn't very nice,' Jordan comments, obviously referring to Wayne's foot.

'Not nice at all,' Wayne agrees. 'You're lucky it's not broken.'

I bet he'll have a big bruise, unless his foot is made of reinforced concrete or something!

Jordan starts tapping his foot. 'We can stop here all night if you like.'

'Yeah. All night.'

It's echo-time again!

'On the other hand,' Jordan continues, 'we could beat the living daylights out of you right here, right now. I'm sure this old geezer won't mind.'

'Even if he does, what could he do anyway?' Dean mocks. 'He looks like he can hardly stand up!'

As if on cue, the old chap gets to his feet. He is unexpectedly tall. Wayne and Dean nearly fall over each other as they back away from him.

The old man peers down at them, smiling. 'Not afraid of someone who can't stand up, are you?' he enquires. Suddenly he doesn't seem so old any more.

The boys struggle to their feet and join Jordan. The three now stand firm together – all for one and one for all! But they seem more like mouse-keteers than musketeers as they stare up at their new foe.

I have no idea what they intend to do, but Jordan is wearing a determined look. He makes a sudden grab for my arm, but then *his* arm is grabbed and he finds himself back where he started.

To my utter confusion, the old man steps forward and sweeps his arm slowly from left to right in front of the terrible trio. He says calmly, almost soothingly: 'I think it's time you were heading home. Your mothers will be worried about you.'

Is he joking? I didn't even know they *had* mothers. They're not going to be happy with the way he's talking to them.

But Jordan and his pals look like three rabbits frozen in somebody's headlights. Their eyes have taken on a steady, empty glare. They've been hypnotized or something!

Like robots, they open their mouths and declare in unison: *'We think it's time we were heading home. Our mothers will be worried about us.'* The voices don't even sound like theirs. It's like they've been possessed.

Perfectly synchronized in their movements, they turn around and head off towards the gates. As they leave the park, they are actually holding hands! They look like they're off somewhere up the Yellow Brick Road like the Scarecrow, Tin Man and Cowardly Lion.

The old man smiles and sits back down.

I am too stunned to speak, but finally manage to say: 'How did you do that?'

'Oh, that,' he says, as if it was nothing. 'Just a little something I saw in a film.'

We sit in silence. I am bewildered. I decide to stay on the bench a bit longer, just to make sure the coast is completely clear. But a few minutes pass by and there's no sign of Jordan, Dean or Wayne. They really must have gone home to their mothers.

The old man turns to me and asks me if I've had a good day in school.

A good day? That's a laugh!

'Hardly,' I reply.

'Hmmm,' he says. What this means I have no idea.

'It's been one of those days,' I explain.

'And what type of days would those be?' he says.

I'm beginning to wonder if he's from this planet.

'One of those days from hell,' I state plainly. 'One of those days when just about everything that *could* go wrong *does* go wrong! From the moment I woke up this morning (half an hour later than I should have) till about five minutes ago, it's been a complete and utter disaster.'

Today has felt like one long row of falling dominoes.

'Hmmm,' he comments, 'some days are like that.'

I hope he doesn't have any more pearls of wisdom up his sleeve.

'That's a great help,' I say. 'Thanks.'

He lets out an explosive laugh, reaches into his jacket pocket and pulls out a packet of sweets. 'I always find a polo helps on occasions like these.' He takes out a polo and holds it in front of him, admiring it as if it's a work of art or something. 'Absolutely perfect,' he declares.

'What? The polo?'

'No, no! The circle. Shape of all shapes. Perfection itself.'

He then puts the polo in his mouth and offers me one. My mother's voice is yelling inside my brain: 'Never take sweets from strangers!' but somehow this old man inspires me with trust. I don't feel in danger at all; in fact, quite the opposite.

I take the offered polo and then we shake hands. He says his name is Lyn.

Lyn? Lyn's a girl's name, I think to myself. It's so refreshing to meet somebody else with an odd name.

He seems to be enjoying his sweet. 'Bet you I can make mine last longer than yours,' he says.

It's about time I was going. 'Look,' I say, 'thanks for the polo, but I'm not really into games.'

Lyn looks taken aback. 'Not interested in games. A boy of your age? What is the world coming to?'

'Didn't I just tell you I've had a bad day today?' My voice is slightly raised.

He turns towards me. 'Listen, young fella,' he says, 'we all get our share of bad days. But we all get our share of good days too. They all balance out. That's what life is all about. It's like that see-saw over there – ups and downs!'

'Well, there's something wrong with my see-saw, because it seems to be going down more than it's going up.'

Lyn pats me on the shoulder. 'Perhaps see-saw is the wrong analogy,' he says. He seems to know a lot of big words. 'More like a rollercoaster. Lots of twists and turns, eh?'

'Too right!' I moan.

'Look,' he laughs, 'you wouldn't want to sit on a see-saw that stays in one position all the time, would you? And you sure as eggs wouldn't want to ride a rollercoaster that crawls constantly upwards and never comes down. Where would be the fun in that?'

This conversation is getting really deep.

'Sounds to me,' he continues, 'as though somebody's feeling sorry for themselves.'

This is the last thing I need at the moment – being preached at by an OAP!

'Look,' I say, staring down at my trainers, 'if you were in my shoes, you'd feel sorry for me too!'

Lyn sighs and stands up. I can hear his knees crack. 'Listen,' he says, 'you're going to get a lot more bad days before your life is over, I can tell you that for a fact. I've had more bad days in *my* life than I'd care to remember, probably more bad days than you've had hot dinners. But I just accept them.'

'Look,' I say, still focusing on my trainers, 'there's bad days and then there's *ba-ad* days! Today has been the pits of the world. I wish I could climb back into bed and start again.'

'I'd be careful what I wish for, if I were you,' he says mysteriously and starts to walk away. Then, as an afterthought: 'Perhaps we'll meet again some time.'

I don't see how. It's been interesting meeting him though. He did save my bacon after all! I call after him: 'Thanks for helping me!'

He doesn't turn back. 'You're very welcome, Artie!'

Artie? How does he know my name? He told me *his* name but I don't remember telling him *mine*!

'Hey!' I call after him, but he speeds up, then suddenly veers from the path, strides across the grass and disappears through a gap in the hedge that I had no idea was there.

I run after him but, when I get to the hedge, there *is* no gap! Certainly not big enough for a man to get through! This is all too weird. I'm starting to feel like Alice in Wonderland chasing the white rabbit down the hole.

I scratch my head. I think I need to go and lie down.

I head for the gates and then notice something lying on the floor next to the bench. It looks like a carrier bag. Lyn must have left his shopping.

I run over to it. If I hurry, I might be able to catch him up.

As I lift it, I realize it's not shopping after all – it's a parcel!

It's covered in expensive-looking wrapping-paper,

with lots of pictures of different types of clocks – grandfather clocks, sundials, hourglasses, pocket watches. It's heavy too!

There's a tag on it and, being nosy, I can't resist having a look.

I nearly drop the bag on my foot.

The message on the tag reads:

To Artie,
Be careful what you wish for!
Lyn

Chapter 4

The Trip

My legs are suddenly feeling like jelly and I slump down on the bench.

I half-expect somebody to jump out of the bushes with a microphone and camera, yelling at me: 'You've been framed!!'

This situation is beyond me!

I've only met this old man, Lyn, about twenty minutes ago and yet he's managed to get a present ready for me, wrapped, labelled and bagged.

And how does he know my name?

I pinch myself just to make sure I'm not dreaming.

Logically, the next thing for me to do is open the present. But I decide I'd much rather do so in the privacy of my own bedroom.

I pick up the parcel and head for home.

As I start walking the last few blocks to my house, there's no sign of Jordan and company – or the old man either!

I feel very strange, very uncomfortable, as though people are watching me, as though it's written all over my face that something weird has just happened to me.

I decide that it's probably best if my mother doesn't see the present. Too many questions! So I bypass the front door, head around the back and hide the bag in the shed.

'Where've you been, luv?' my mum calls out. The back door's open and she's in the kitchen. The windows are all steamed up.

I need an excuse. 'Uh – Mr Batty wanted some help tidying up the class.'

'Do you realize it's nearly quarter past four? Didn't you think I'd be worried? Anyway, I thought you didn't like Mr Batty.'

I wish I'd thought this through now. 'I-I-I-I . . .'

'I-I-I-I . . ?' she mocks

'I – he can be all right – sometimes.'

She's in the middle of mashing some potatoes in this huge saucepan, but stops for a second and looks at me quizzically. Then she smiles and says: 'You're a strange one.'

'I know,' I agree, give her a peck on the cheek and scoot upstairs to change my clothes.

'Don't hang about! Tea's nearly ready!' she calls after me.

I sit on my bed, trying to work out how I am going to smuggle the bag upstairs. My mum has eagle-eyes. I'm amazed she didn't see me sneaking into the shed!

But then I remember what day it is. It's Monday! And Mum always goes to aerobics on Mondays, from six till seven. Perfect!

I'm getting quite excited. I have no idea what the present could be.

'Tea's ready, luv!'

Woh! That was quick!

'I'm coming!' I yell, rapidly swapping my uniform for jeans and sweatshirt.

I clatter down the stairs, nearly breaking my foot on one of Sali's dolls and land in a heap at the bottom.

'Do you have to be so noisy?' Mum calls out. 'You sound like a herd of elephants.'

I pick myself up. Check for injuries. Fortunately nothing is broken. Sali's doll looks the worse for wear, though! Its head is facing the wrong way and looks like something out of a Goosebumps book! I admire the improvement.

'Herd of what . . ?' I say, strolling into the kitchen.

'Herd of elephants.'

'Heard of elephants? Of course I've heard of elephants.' She'll never know that I've just had one of the worst days of my eleven-year-old life.

'All right, clever clogs. Sit down, your food's ready.'

Sali is already sitting down, two cushions underneath her so she can reach the table.

I sit down and start eating my fish-fingers, peas and mashed potatoes, but the mash is too powdery and dry so I get up to fetch some tomato ketchup.

'Where are you going *now*?' Mum asks impatiently.

'Tomato sauce,' I explain.

'There *isn't* any. Sali's just had the last of it.'

Great.

I look at Sali. Specifically, I look at her mashed potatoes, which are not creamy-white, but orange. She must have used up at least half a bottle in there! The rest of the sauce is splattered over the tablecloth and her hair!

'That's just great!' I comment. 'I love dry food.'

'Well, have a drink of water then, and stop moaning. Anyway, if you'd been home on time, there would have been some tomato sauce left.'

Why do grown-ups have an answer for everything?

I feel a sudden splatter of orange mashed-potato on my nose and left cheek.

A present from Sali!

'Can you sort her out, Mum!' I yell, wiping the food from my face.

Mum has a fit of the giggles. 'She's only trying to share her tomato sauce with you.'

Yeah. Right.

Mum runs a dishcloth under the tap and starts wiping all the gunk off Sali. Don't worry about *me*, Mum. I'll be fine.

With her back to me, Mum asks me the daily question, the question that she doesn't really want to know the answer to: 'So, what kind of day have you had, Art?'

'Fine, thanks,' I say, as she continues cleaning up Sali's mess. 'I was told off and humiliated for being late, I forgot my homework, I got sent out of assembly for something I didn't do, I got in trouble at dinner-time, I got dropped from the baseball squad . . . and the girl I fancy hates my guts. Oh, and just to top it all, Jordan Bates and his two pals will probably kill me the next time they catch sight of me.'

'Sounds great,' Mum comments as she wipes up the red sea of ketchup on the tablecloth. She then starts washing up.

She hasn't heard a word I've just said. Well. I'm certainly not saying it all again!

I give Sali a menacing glare and then try and swallow some of my food.

My thoughts return to Lyn's present. What could it be? Some play-station games would be nice, or some DVDs – *Lord of the Rings* is my favourite! Anyway, I'll be finding out soon enough.

'Oh, by the way,' says Mum, turning round from her washing-up, 'I need you to do me a huge favour. I need you to babysit Sali for an hour while I nip over to my aerobics class. I don't like asking you but . . .'

'It's OK,' I say. 'You can go. We'll be fine.' After all, it's only an hour. What can possibly go wrong in an hour? And, in any case, I need to examine Lyn's present.

'Thanks, luv,' she says, coming over to me and grabbing my cheeks with her foamy hands. 'You're my little knight in shining armour.'

'OK, OK,' I say, pushing her away.

I struggle to get the rest of my food down my throat, then go upstairs to play *Dark Warriors* on my play-station. It's my favourite swords-and-sorcery game. And I'm really good at it. I've only got one more level to achieve.

Ninety minutes fly by and, before I know it, there's a knock on my bedroom door. 'I'm just going, luv.'

'OK,' I say, reluctantly surrendering the digital battle.

'Now, promise me that you won't take your eyes off her. I'll be back just after seven.'

'Yes, Mum.'

I follow her down the stairs. She opens the front door, gives me a peck on the cheek, and then heads off to the Community Centre, which is directly opposite our house.

She gets as far as the pavement when I call out: 'What am I supposed to do with her?'

She puts her hands on her hips. 'Oh, come on. It's only an hour. Stick a video on or something. She likes *Barbie and the Nutcracker*.'

The road is clear so she takes the opportunity to cross.

Barbie and the Nutcracker!

If there is one film guaranteed to get on my nerves, it's *Barbie and the Nutcracker*! Sali must have watched it about fifty-seven times. Barbie dolls are bad enough, but, when you've got them in widescreen, on your telly, dancing to classical music . . . it's enough to do your head in.

As I enter the living-room, Sali is nowhere to be seen.

'Sali?' I call.

I search under the coffee-table and behind the settee. A giggling sound escapes from behind the curtains. Sali screeches 'Boo!' at me as I pull them back. Don't three-year-olds get on your nerves?

'Listen, Sal,' I say, getting down on my knees. 'Mum says we can watch a video. What about *Lord of the Rings* with funny Gollum in? You know you like that one.'

Sali starts jumping up and down, like she's on a pogo-stick.

'No!' she yells. '*Barbie!*'

'What about *Dungeons and Dragons*?' I suggest. 'You like dragons.'

More jumping. 'Nuh-uh! *Barbie!*'

'*The Sword in the Stone*?'

'*Barbie*! *Barbie*! *Barbie*!'

This is the kind of logical argument you get from a three-year-old.

'OK, OK,' I mutter.

I search through our video cabinet but can't find it. Thank you, God!

'It's not here, Sal.' I break the sad news.

She points over my shoulder at the telly. 'There! There!'

Unfortunately she's right. It's sitting there, right next to the telly, in its bright pink and lilac cover.

Game, set and match to Sali, I guess!

I reluctantly set the video up and press 'play'. Sali instantly enters a sort of Barbie-world trance.

I sit on our only armchair, keeping both my eyes on my sister, as I'd promised. After a few minutes of this, boredom sets in and I entertain myself by waving my hand in front of Sali's face. She doesn't even blink!

Now would be a good time to nip out into the shed and get the present.

But what if something happens to Sali while I'm gone?

Like what?

What could she possibly get up to in one minute? Fall off the settee?

I make up my mind to go for it. She won't even know I'm gone.

I ease myself gently off the chair, trying not to make any sudden movements. I start crawling towards the door. I must look ridiculous.

Then I freeze.

Sali is muttering something. Perhaps talking to Barbie. Or the nutcracker!

But no. She's talking to me.

'I need a wee,' she declares.

I stand up, looking like an idiot. 'But you went ten minutes ago.'

Sali is already off the settee and grabbing my hand.

'You know where the bathroom is,' I say, trying to escape from her hand, but she won't let go and leads me, like a dog on a lead, to the bottom of the stairs.

'I know,' I say. 'As you're such a big girl, I'll wait here and I'll count and see how long you take.'

This game seems to appeal to Sali and she starts clambering up the stairs.

I helpfully switch the upstairs light on and start counting, loudly: 'ONE BANANA . . . TWO BANANAS . . . THREE BANANAS . . . FOUR BANANAS . . . FIVE . . .'

I get to about twelve and then abandon my counting. It's now or never! I rocket through the kitchen, nip out the back-door into the shed, feel for the carrier-bag behind the hose-pipe, snatch it up and pelt back to the bottom of the stairs. The road-runner couldn't have done it any faster! *Meep meep!*

I take up the counting again: 'EIGHTEEN BANANAS . . . NINETEEN BANANAS . . . TWENTY BANANAS . . .'

I get to thirty-nine bananas. No sign of Sali.

'Are you all right?' I bellow up the stairs.

'It won't come!' is the reply.

'Well, just wait there until it does!' Perhaps the counting has put her off.

Now seems like a good opportunity.

I lift the present out of the bag, feel its weight and hardness, read the label again.

It's all so weird!

There's a loud thud from above. I look up. Sali has just bounded onto the top stair.

'Be careful,' I tell her. 'Did you wash your hands?'

Nod of the head.

She starts to walk down the stairs and . . . trips!

And screams!

I feel like my heart is falling with her. I want to scream too!

As if in slow-motion, she tumbles awkwardly towards me, banging her head on the way down.

The parcel falls from my grasp as I lurch forward to try and catch her . . .

Chapter 5

Present and Past

And then a miracle takes place.

Sali is about three-quarters of the way down the stairs, tumbling and screaming, when she comes to an abrupt halt, mid-air, and then switches into reverse, tumbles *up* the stairs (even screaming in reverse!) and disappears onto the landing!

I feel like an idiot, standing there with my arms outstretched, ready to catch her. A relieved idiot, though!

What just happened?

Then there's a sudden loud thud from above.

Sali bounds onto the top stair – for the second time in the last sixty seconds!

'Be careful . . .' I start to say, and then shoot up the stairs, two steps at a time. I catch her, mid-fall.

'Wheeeeeee!' she squeals, obviously thinking it's a game. 'More! More!'

Not likely!

I hold on to her tight, my heart beating like a little bird's.

On rubbery legs, I somehow manage to carry her to the sofa and back into the world of Barbie. I flop down into the armchair and try to come to terms with what's just happened. My eyes stay firmly fixed on Sali. I'm determined she's not going anywhere.

What the heck is going on?

The day started off badly but now it's gone completely freaky!

I sit in a state of shock and wait for my mother to come home. And, at just after seven, right on schedule, the front door opens.

'Everything all right, luv?'

'Yeah.' Everything's absolutely wonderful! Sali just fell up and down the stairs but, apart from that, everything is just dandy!

'What's this?' Mum calls out.

My heart skips a beat.

'What's what?'

For one minute, I think she's found some blood on the stairs!

'This parcel!'

Uh-oh. I've been sitting in this chair for the last half-an-hour and the blinking present's been sitting at the bottom of the stairs! How could I have forgotten about it?

What am I supposed to say?

'Oh, that,' I explain. 'It's a birthday present.'

'For who?'

'For me.'

Laughter from the hallway. 'Yours? In case you'd forgotten, your birthday's in December, and it's now April.'

'I know. It's a *late* birthday present.' I'm really struggling now!

'Late?' she says, popping her head into the living-room. 'You're not joking!'

And then she looks at the label. 'Who's Lyn?'

Here goes. 'She's a girl in my class.'

'Ooooh!' she smirks. 'A girl!'

She turns her attention back to the parcel in her hands. 'Feels heavy,' she comments. 'What is it?'

Duh! I haven't opened it yet.

'Dunno.'

'Well, let's have a look, then!' she says, passing it over to me. She looks quite excited. 'A girl, eh?'

Sali's voice comes sailing over from the settee. 'I need a poo.' What *she* needs is a season-ticket for the bathroom!

Mum's reaction is immediate. She forgets about me and the present and goes over to pick Sali up. 'Come on then, stinky!' And they're gone.

It's just me and the present now.

There's no longer any need to hesitate.

I rip the paper off.

I don't know what I was expecting – but it's not what lies in front of me!

It's a tape-recorder.

I have no idea why Lyn might think I need one of these.

I examine it closely. It doesn't look modern at all; it looks like one my Dad showed me which he'd had when he was little.

It's about the same size and weight as an encyclopaedia – really chunky!

It's black all over; it has one cassette compartment

and six labelled buttons: RECORD, FORWARD, PLAY, REWIND, STOP/EJECT and PAUSE.

As I'm looking at it, it strikes me that it's second-hand. It's got dust on it and it's covered in scratches. There's even a speck of what looks like white paint!

I sit there, mulling over all the facts, like a detective investigating a case: an old man I've never met before rescues me from some thugs; he has a present waiting for me, pre-wrapped and labelled; it turns out to be a second-hand tape-recorder . . .

I'm at a complete loss.

'What is it, then?' enquires my mum as she carries Sali back into the room.

I hold it up and show her.

'Oh. That's nice,' she comments. She can't see the condition it's in. 'Why don't you try it out?'

This is going to be difficult. I haven't actually got any audio-cassettes. CDs yes. Tapes no.

As if reading my mind, Mum says: 'I think *I've* got a tape in there.' She points to the sideboard drawers.

I get up and have a look. There's only one tape. It's called *Greatest Hits of the Eighties* and has bands called *Spandau Ballet* and *Duran Duran* on it. There's no accounting for taste!

I sit back down, pop the cassette into the machine and press the 'play' button.

Nothing.

No sound. No movement.

Mum laughs. 'It might help if you plugged it in, dopey!'

Sometimes I can be so stupid!

I place the recorder down on the carpet near the socket in the wall, plug it in, put the switch on and push the 'play' button.

Nothing.

Absolutely nothing.

Great! Not only have I just been given a second-hand present, but it's a second-hand present that doesn't work.

A perfect end to a perfect day!

I let out a sigh, pick up my 'present' and slope off to my bedroom, mumbling something about homework.

'Artie?' my mother says, but I'm gone.

I drag myself up the stairs and collapse in a defeated heap on the bed.

I stare up at my ceiling.

My *red* ceiling.

I've been living with this ceiling ever since my dad left four years ago. I told him I wanted Man United colours, but I never expected him to paint the walls white and the ceiling red! He said it was perfectly logical – Man United's shorts are white and their tops are red. So the walls represent their shorts and the ceiling represents their tops. Logical, eh? My dad has some funny ideas. *Had* some funny ideas.

I lie on my back, hands behind my head, pondering the day's events. I'm starting to doubt my own senses. Did I really see Sali fall down the stairs and then shoot back up again?

I sit up and pick up the tape-recorder again. I was holding this when Sali tripped. Then I dropped it and she started reversing up the stairs.

I couldn't see any connection.

It's just a tatty old tape-recorder!

But why would an old man give me something if it was completely useless? Why be so cruel? Lyn didn't seem like a mean person; in fact, quite the opposite.

I press the buttons, one by one:

RECORD   Nothing.
FORWARD   Nothing.
PLAY   Nothing.
REWIND   Something . . .

I notice that the set of numbers above the buttons has started moving. They're counting – backwards.

A sinking sensation develops in my stomach and then all the furniture in my room starts moving! It's as if everything's melting. I feel like I'm in a piece of pavement art that's been exposed to the rain, all the colours and shapes running into each other.

I start to panic and quickly press the button again.

To my utter confusion, I find myself in the living-room, sitting in the armchair, staring at Sali.

The tape-recorder has vanished!

A voice sounds out from the hallway. 'Everything all right, luv?'

'Yeah. Fine,' I say, without giving it much thought.

'What's this?' Mum calls out, just like she did ten minutes ago.

'What's what?'

This conversation is sounding very familiar.

'This parcel.'

Dumbfounded silence from me.

'Is anyone there?' calls Mum. 'Earth calling Artie!'

My brain clicks into gear again. 'It's a birthday present from a . . . from a girl in my class called Lyn and, before you say, I know it's four months late.'

'Ooh, a girl!'

Entering the room, she starts fingering the parcel. 'It's heavy. What is it?'

'It's a tape-recorder,' I can now state with confidence.

'How do you know?'

Because I opened it ten minutes ago!

'Because Lyn told me what it was. It's not a *real* present.'

Mum hands me the parcel with a look of total bewilderment.

There's quite a lot of things that *I* don't understand right now!

Unless I'm completely losing my marbles, hitting the 'rewind' button on this tape-recorder makes time go backwards!

I've just gone back in time ten minutes!

Cool!

And when I dropped the recorder in the hallway, the 'rewind' button must have connected with the bottom step. I vaguely remember it bouncing.

Sali's voice drifts over. 'I need a poo.'

Mum sighs, picks Sali up and heads for the bathroom.

Quicker than you can say 'fast forward', I grab my present and zip back up the stairs to my room.

Things are starting to look up!

This is not such a useless present, after all!

Chapter 6

Bobbing Along . . .

Where had Lyn got the tape-recorder from?

You certainly can't buy anything like this at your local electrical store.

This tacky-looking lump of black plastic is actually a . . . time-machine!

And, as far as I know, time-machines haven't been invented yet.

And some scientists think they never *will* be invented!

Because time-travel is *impossible*!

This is incredible!

I look at my little time-machine. What shall I do with it?

There are so many possibilities.

Perhaps I can visit the Victorians and help the police catch Jack the Ripper. Or go to Tudor times, meet Henry the Eighth and watch his wives have their heads chopped off! Or visit the Roman period and see some real gladiators! Or travel far, far, far back in time and see how scary T-Rexes really were! Or maybe not!

I start thinking about my *own* life, my *own* history.

I've got the chance here to re-live some really cool moments. I must admit I have had some.

Like the time when Mrs Lewis asked me to read my story out to the whole class, because she thought it was so funny! It was about a group of incompetent aliens who try to invade our planet but make a mess of it. I remember Callum Young falling off his chair when one of the aliens walks up to a petrol-pump and says: 'Take me to your leader!'

And then I realize that, in fact, I haven't got *that* many great moments to re-live.

What I've got is a lot of *bad* moments that I'd like to change!

Like the time I blu-tacked a drawing-pin to Rhys Williams's chair. He completely over-reacted and hopped around the room like his bum was on fire! I got into major trouble over that.

Or the time I thought it was funny to hide Jayne Inglesson's sandwiches in Lewis Roberts's bag. What was I thinking?

Or the time when I told Mr Batty to stop picking on me and give someone else a turn. (My mouth is probably my worst enemy.)

Or . . . THE WHOLE OF TODAY!

Not a bad idea.

Maybe I can turn today completely around.

Change it into a perfect day.

Given a second chance, I can do all the right things, say all the right things, make all the right moves.

I can get to school on time. I can stay away from Callum Young during assembly. I can stay cool at lunchtime and on the baseball field. I can avoid Jordan Bates and his gang by leaving school on time . . .

Boy, I am *so* looking forward (or is it backward?) to this.

But when to do it?

Why not now? I'm not doing anything important.

I need to be ready, though.

I sit cross-legged, like the Buddha on the RE poster in the library. Only not so fat!

The tape-recorder sits in front of me.

My finger creeps cautiously towards the 'rewind' button.

And then quickly retreats again. I need to think about this.

This is a big deal!

I've seen these films where characters go back in time, and every little change they make in the past affects the future. I'm starting to wonder if pressing the button is such a good idea after all.

But why was I given this blinking tape-recorder if I'm not supposed to use it?

Unless Lyn is up to no good, of course!

I find this hard to imagine. If he's not a good person, then neither is Father Christmas!

And even if I do press the button, how long am I supposed to press it for? I'd like to go back to about eight o'clock this morning – that's about twelve hours ago.

Earlier on, I'd pressed it for about five seconds and gone back ten minutes. Does that mean one second equals two minutes? Thirty seconds equals one hour. So I'd have to press the button for six minutes to go back twelve hours!

Six minutes!!! That's a long time!

And how can I stop myself going too far?

I can't believe I'm being such a wimp. I can fight hordes of rampaging Picts in my head, but, in real life, I can't even press a simple button.

I can feel myself getting angry with my own indecisiveness. Anything's got to be an improvement!

I reach over to my radio-alarm and set it to go off in six minutes, then sit up straight again and press the 'rewind' button.

It clicks into position and stays down.

The numbers on the clock-counter start going backwards rapidly – faster than before, unless I'm imagining it!

Just like before, my stomach starts to turn over, as if I'm falling down a tunnel.

Just like before, everything, including my Man United walls and ceiling, starts to melt.

My bed is going all fuzzy and then, without warning, it sinks through the floor with me still on it.

I find myself in the living-room. I can just about see Sali and Mum on the sofa, but they're fuzzy-looking too! They don't seem to be aware of me!

The bed is jiggling all over the place.

It seems to have taken on a life of its own.

Suddenly, it jolts forward – through the gap in Mum's floral curtains and through the wall, like it's not even there!

I find myself out on the street – on my bed!

It's like that film *Bedknobs and Broomsticks*, where the bed travels through the streets of foggy London and then bobs along on the bottom of the 'beautiful briny sea'.

Here I am, bobbing along Monnow Way, in Bettws, South Wales!

Once again I pinch myself – very hard.

No, it's not a dream!

I glance down at the tape-recorder – the numbers are still reversing.

My radio-alarm is back in the bedroom though!

There are some teenagers walking half on the pavement, half off. They're walking very fast and they're walking backwards! They don't seem to notice me as I nearly run them over in my bed-mobile!

Cars and buses come towards me and from behind me, but they go right through me as if I'm a ghost.

The sun is rising abnormally quickly in the sky.

We head up a side-street towards the park. The gates are far too narrow for the bed to get through! I close my eyes and hang on tight, waiting for a collision.

But the gates present no problem. After all, we've just been through cars, buses and a brick wall!

The clock-counter seems to be speeding up.

We shoot through the gates and career about the park: under the slide, through the swings, round the roundabout a few times. The bed is acting like an excited puppy. It's obviously never been in a park before!

And then, abruptly, everything slows down. I can see Lyn sitting on the bench, reading a newspaper. He puts the paper down and waves at me. His head follows my slow passage past him. It feels like we're at Wimbledon, Lyn is the only spectator – and I'm the ball, travelling in slow-motion.

I wave back.

And then I'm suddenly jolted against the headboard as the bed picks up speed again, shoots out of the park and heads towards my school.

According to the clock-counter, the 'rewind' button has been down for two minutes now.

I can just make out Jordan Bates, Wayne and Dean standing, skittle-like, at the school-gates. We're heading straight for them and the bed is showing no signs of slowing down. If only I was a *real* bowling-ball and they were three skittles! KA-BOOM!!!

Of course, we pass straight through them!

Shame.

The bed flies down the five flights of steps, makes a quick visit to Mr Griffiths's office and then heads out towards the field.

The sun is even higher in the sky now and still rising.

I feel like I'm on a fairground-ride – an out-of-control fairground-ride!

We start whizzing around the field, in and out of the baseball-players. It's almost as if the bed is chasing after them, joining in the fun. *It* is obviously enjoying itself, but *I'm* starting not to.

I'm feeling dizzy now, and a little bit sick. And the numbers on the tape-recorder have become a blur! The events of the day continue to run backwards, faster and faster.

The sinking sensation is back, with a vengeance!
I feel like I'm being sucked down a plug-hole!

Round and round and round she goes,

where she stops, nobody knows

round and round

and down and down . . .

and round . . . and down . . .

. . . and down . . . and round

. . . and down

. . . and down . . .

. . . and down . . .

Chapter 7

Play it Again . . .

'Arrtttiieeeeee!!! Wake up!!! You're going to be late again!!!'

My eyes open. I don't even remember closing them. I must have passed out. I'm lying on my bed – correction, *in* my bed – in my bedroom. I lift up the sheets. I've got my pyjamas on! I sit up with a start, and fumble about for the tape-recorder.

I can't find it. Either that, or it's not here!

'It's half past eight!' my mother calls out.

What!!??

I'm going to be late! Again!

I fall out of bed and stagger into the next room, where Mum is struggling to get a t-shirt on Sali, a t-shirt with buttons!

'Mum, what day is it?' I mumble, scratching my head.

She stops struggling with Sali. 'What *day* is it? What day do you *think* it is? Yesterday was Sunday, so that makes today Monday. And tomorrow's Tuesday! Really Artie!'

'Just checking.'

So it's worked then. I've just gone back in time, twelve hours! I don't know how the tape-recorder managed to stop itself rewinding, but it must have done, because here I am!

I'd better get a move on if I don't want the re-run of my day to be exactly the same as the original. I do *not* want to be late for school again! I scramble into my clothes and grab a chewing gum from my bedside table. No time to brush my teeth – or have breakfast, for that matter!

I run at breakneck speed along Monnow Way, sidestepping occasionally for dogs, small children and old ladies. I nearly put the postman on his back! As I'm running, my mind is swirling with thoughts about the day that lies ahead of me. It's going to be so cool!

It'll be like being in a play. I'll know what all the other characters are going to say and do! But I'm the only one who's allowed to change the script. So, as well as being one of the actors, I'll be the director too!

This doesn't feel like *real* life any more. I can have some fun with it. Perhaps I don't need to be on my best behaviour! I can have a laugh instead. After all, at precisely four o'clock, if I go to the park, an old man called Lyn will give me a tape-recorder, and I can restart the whole day again if I need to.

I stop running and get my breath back. There's five minutes until the whistle. I can be on time if I *want* to. But I'm no longer sure that I *do* want to.

I saunter the rest of the way to school and then pause at the gates. I can see the yard from here. Most of the 'angels' are already on the yard; some keen ones have already lined up.

Lewis Roberts comes running up behind me.

'Wow!' he says, looking at his watch. 'You're on time! Why are you hanging about here?'

'Just chillin',' I explain.

A teacher's whistle pierces the air. It's nine o'clock.

'Gotta go!' Lewis declares and sets off, bounding down the school steps.

I hunker down behind the hedge and spend ten minutes watching an ant travel from my left trainer to my right trainer and back again.

At 9.10 precisely, I decide it's time for school.

I boldly swagger past Mr Griffiths's open window, singing at the top of my voice:

I'm late, I'm late
For a very important date
No time to say hello, goodbye,
I'm late, I'm late, I'm LATE!!!

But the office is empty! I stroll through the hall without meeting anyone. Our classroom door stands wide open, as do the possibilities that lie before me!

I can do what I want. I can literally get away with murder, if I want to, without any fear of consequences. When today is finished, I can just rub it out and start again!

I nip back to the cloakroom, pick up a pink glove that's lying on the floor, put it on, take my trainers off, put them on the wrong feet and then hobble into the classroom.

Mr Batty only looks up because some of the girls are giggling.

He has no idea what lies in store for him!

'Ah, Mr King,' he says. 'How nice of you to join us. *Prynhawn da!*'

'Thank you, sir,' I say grandly, taking a bow. 'And a

very good afternoon to you too, sir.' I can do sarcasm too! I've learned from a master!

'Late again,' he mutters. 'Doesn't that bus of yours ever run on time?'

Shows how much he knows about me. I *never* catch a bus.

'No, sir. Actually, it runs on petrol. Or is it diesel? I can't remember.'

A few gasps from my classmates, a few surprised giggles.

I shuffle as slowly as I can to my desk, drawing a lot of attention to myself. Out of the corner of my eye, I can see Mr Batty getting agitated, tapping his pen on his desk repeatedly.

He suddenly pushes his chair back and stands up. 'Look at you,' he bellows, 'a tortoise could move faster! What do you think you're doing?'

I stop shuffling, cup my chin in my right hand. 'About two miles an hour, I should think, sir.'

Rhys Williams collapses with laughter.

'Be quiet, Rhys!'

'Yes, sir.'

I resume my shuffling.

Mr Batty looks bemused. 'Why on earth are you walking like that? Are you planning to join the circus or something?'

'No, sir. My trainers hurt.'

He looks at me in disbelief. 'Of course they hurt, they're on the wrong feet.'

I look down, pretending to be puzzled. 'But, sir, *these* are the only feet I've got.'

Roars of laughter!

Mr Batty's face is turning a beautiful shade of purple. 'Put them on properly. And, while you're at it, take that glove off. What's it for anyway?'

He has fallen nicely into my trap. I hold my hands in the air. The left one has a bright pink glove on it. 'Well, sir, I looked at the weather-report last night and the weatherman said that on the *one* hand it might be hot, but on the *other* hand it might be cold.'

Slam-dunk!! That's about three-nil to me, I should think.

I'm expecting Mr Batty to go bananas but, for some reason, he doesn't. He just tells me to sit down and goes back to his dinner register.

The next hour passes fairly quietly. I don't get the opportunity to say anything witty, because 'sir' has obviously decided he doesn't want to talk to me! This is odd, because he normally has a go at me at least once every twenty minutes. This isn't like him at all.

To be quite honest, he looks a bit tired. Perhaps he's not well.

The bell rings for assembly.

My original intention was to sit as far away from Callum Young as possible, to avoid trouble, but now I have quite different ideas! I plonk myself down right next to him.

Halfway through the prayer, as expected, Callum lifts up his fore-arm, nearly elbowing me in the face, takes a deep breath, puts his mouth to his arm and then creates this unbelievably loud noise. From where

Mr Griffiths is sitting, it probably sounds like somebody has broken wind.

Stunned silence in the hall.

Except from me.

I stand up and start clapping. As if Callum has just given a tremendous musical performance.

'Bravo! Bravo!' I exclaim grandly. 'And, pray tell us, Mr Young, can you play any other musical instruments?'

Callum's face now matches his red jersey, much to my satisfaction. He glares at me with dagger-eyes.

He's not the only one looking at me. Two hundred pairs of eyes are staring in my direction. The Year Fives are gazing at me as if I've completely lost my marbles!

'King and Young, leave us,' announces Mr Griffiths calmly.

'But, sir,' I protest, '*I* didn't do anything!'

'You disrupted my assembly, thank you very much.'

'You're welcome.'

'I'm *what*!!!'

'You're welcome, sir.'

Mr Griffiths puts down his book of assembly stories. 'King, you've got about ten seconds to get outside my office.'

'But, sir. He's the one that made the noise!' I protest, pointing at Callum, who looks like he wants the ground to swallow him up.

'And *you're* the one that drew attention to something that could have been ignored.'

Ignored? Ignored? How could anyone ignore *that*? It was like a volcano erupting.

Callum starts walking, so I follow. It's like a game of follow-my-leader.

He throws himself onto the chair outside the office. I have to grab another one from the canteen. I don't sit too near him; he is *not* a happy bunny!

'I'm gonna get you for this, King!' he hisses.

'That's nice, watcha gonna get me?'

'If you had brains you'd be dangerous!'

'Who let you out of your cage then?'

Callum is out of his seat, but luckily Mr Taylor arrives to sit with us. He sits down opposite us, takes a newspaper out of his jacket pocket and starts reading. Callum glares at me.

Ten minutes later, Mr Griffiths arrives.

'Right, you two. In you go!'

Mr Griffiths sits on the edge of his desk, next to his potted plant. He addresses Callum first.

'Young,' he says, 'do you have any explanation for your behaviour in the hall?'

'Yes, sir. I was just trying to blow something off my arm and this sound just sort of came out of my mouth.'

Came out? You've got to be joking! There was enough force behind that raspberry to knock down the Great Wall of China!

'That's very hard to believe, Callum. You showed a complete lack of respect for everyone else in the hall. As a result, you can miss morning play tomorrow.'

'But, sir . . .'

'Off you go, back to class.'

Callum mopes off, giving me a sly kick on the way out.

Mr Griffiths turns his attention to me. 'King, I don't know what's the matter with you lately.'

I yawn loudly. Really loudly. 'Don't you, sir? Perhaps it's time you retired!'

Have I gone too far?

Probably! Mr Griffiths's face is a picture! The veins in the side of his head are throbbing like little blue worms.

He stands up and puts his face about two centimetres from mine. 'How dare you, you insolent boy! I don't mind telling you, I have *never* been spoken to like that in *all* my years of teaching!'

If I was wearing a wig, it would be about two metres behind me right now, such is the force of Mr Griffiths's bellowing!

'You mean, not since 1896, sir? Zowee, that's a long time!'

His hand reaches for his phone, like a gunfighter reaching for his Colt 45. 'Right, I think it's about time we had a word with your mother. Let's see what she has to say.'

'She'll probably say "Hello". No, come to think of it, she probably won't say anything at all. She's gone shopping for the day in Cardiff.'

Mr Griffiths slams the phone down. 'It's not important,' he says. 'You can take a letter home tonight, explaining why you've been excluded for the rest of this week!'

I rub my hands together and do a little jig. 'Cool!' I declare. 'I could do with a holiday.'

Mr Griffiths, obviously determined to have the last word, says: 'I don't know what you're so happy about. One more episode like that and you'll be permanently excluded!'

'Sounds painful, sir.'

'Get out of my sight!' he bellows, pointing at the doorway.

I pause for a few seconds. 'Am I dismissed then, sir?'

'Yes, you . . . '

I can't actually hear the rest of the sentence but I am pretty sure it includes a swear word. I don't believe it! Mr Griffiths, swearing? Boy, I must have made him really mad! I have never seen him this angry before.

I leave the office. Hopefully, Mr Griffiths will return to his normal colour in a few minutes.

It's break-time. Time to go and see Gwyneth and her charming chums on the field.

'How ya doin', ladies?' I declare, swaggering up to them.

'Did somebody say something?' says Clare, like I'm invisible or something.

'I didn't hear anything,' says Rachel.

They have their backs to me now.

I pounce forward, step between them and put my arms around them as if we're all best buddies! Then I scream at the top of my voice until they're both forced to pull away and put their hands over their ears.

I shout after them: 'Did you hear THAT!!??'

I can see Gwyneth struggling not to smile. I don't know why she hangs around with these two. They're like the two ugly sisters to her Cinderella. I don't mean that they're bad-looking, because they're not, but, personality-wise, they're hideous!

Clare walks up to me and pokes me hard in the chest. 'Can't you see she doesn't want to talk to you.'

I poke her right back. 'And can't *you* see that you're ugly, nasty and evil and Gwyneth's better off without you? Why don't you go and stir your cauldron or something and leave her alone!'

I watch Gwyneth's hand go to her mouth, partly from shock, I think, and partly to stop herself giggling.

'She likes hanging about with us, moron,' says Rachel.

'*Don't* you, Gwyneth?' says Clare.

To my surprise and, no doubt, to Clare's and Rachel's, Gwyneth doesn't answer. She just sort of shrugs her shoulders.

'Oh, right, I see,' says Clare. She grabs Rachel by the arm and the pair of them storm off.

Gwyneth is left standing alone – with me.

I feel a bit guilty. 'Sorry about that.'

She stares down at the grass. 'That's OK.'

There's an awkward silence while both of us try and think of something to say.

But before we can say anything, Mrs Bowen blows the whistle for end-of-break.

We line up with the rest of the class.

Mr Griffiths has obviously had no luck contacting my mother; otherwise I'd be on my way home by now.

Chapter 8

Put to the Test

Back in class, it's time for science revision . . . 'Only six weeks to go now to those lovely end-of-year tests that you're all looking forward to.'

'Ten pence, sir.'

'Thank you, Rhys. What would I do without you?'

£5.30 in the cookie-jar.

Mr Batty is about to bring up the topic of homework. I decide to get in first and stand up.

'Sit down, King.'

'Sir,' I ask, faking innocence. 'Would you punish me for something I hadn't done?'

Mr Batty looks puzzled. 'No, King, I wouldn't. I know you think I'm some sort of monster, but even *I'm* not that bad.'

'Oh, that's all right then, sir, because I haven't done my homework.'

Guffaws from my class-mates, particularly the boys.

'Very funny. What's your excuse then?'

'Well, that depends, sir. I can't exactly remember *which* homework I'm supposed to have done. If it's the *gravity* homework, I dropped it on the way to school; and if you mean the *digestive system* homework, the dog ate it.'

Mr Batty seems confused. 'I've said it before, King,

and I'll say it again. You don't deserve to be in our school.'

'Thank you, sir.' I take a bow. No applause, though.

I rummage in my pocket and pull out a tatty piece of kitchen-roll. 'I was only joking, sir,' I say, holding it up for him to see. '*Here's* my homework . . .'

Mr Batty frowns at it. 'Am I allowed to ask why it's on a piece of kitchen-roll?'

'Well, sir, I thought you might find it more *absorbing*.'

I can see Gwyneth laughing at this one.

Mr Batty snatches the kitchen-roll off me and looks at it in disgust. There isn't any homework on it, but there *is* a drawing of some cows, which I'd prepared earlier.

'What *is* this?'

'Oh that,' I say, 'that's just a bunch of cows.'

'*Herd* of cows,' Mr Batty corrects me.

'Of course I've *heard* of cows, sir. Do you think I'm stupid or something?'

I just *love* this joke. It's one of my all-time favourites.

Mr Batty looks tired. *Sick* and tired. Of me!

He addresses the class. 'Listen, 6B. King here may well be laughing right here, right now. But I can assure you that he won't be laughing tonight, when his mother hears that he has been excluded tomorrow and Wednesday *and* the rest of the week.'

A gasp from the audience.

'And now,' Mr Batty continues, 'if you don't mind, King, *some* of us have to get ready for our important tests.'

'Ten pence, sir!' shouts the ever-observant Rhys Williams.

'Yes, yes. Thank you, Rhys.'

£5.40. Ker-ching!

Mr Batty really *does* look tired. I almost feel sorry for him.

Almost.

Lunchtime finds me in my favourite spot, under a willow tree, right next to the dell. But not alone this time. Gwyneth has joined me. Rachel and Clare have abandoned her.

We actually start talking to each other. And find we have a lot in common: neither of us has a dad living at home; we both have three-year-old sisters; and we are both interested in animals. Gwyneth has a guinea-pig called Gus and a rabbit called Harvey – and I have a sister called Sali!

I find it easy to talk to Gwyneth. It feels as though I have known her a long, long time, but she only moved to Bettws last year after her parents split up.

We're chatting away merrily when there's a tap on my shoulder.

I ignore it.

'Somebody wants you,' says Gwyneth, pointing behind me.

'Let me guess,' I say, without turning around, 'Gavin Price.'

Gwyneth looks impressed with my psychic powers.

'Oy!' declares this insistent little voice from behind me.

'All right, squirt,' I declare. 'Mrs Moss wants to see me, right?''

'Uh?'

Snotty little Gavin looks confused. It doesn't take much!

'She wants you . . .'

'. . . right away?' I finish his sentence.

This is all far too spooky for Gavin, who makes a quick departure.

'That's amazing,' comments Gwyneth. 'Are you psychic or something?'

'I might be,' I smile. The man of mystery! 'I'll see you later!'

Off I jaunt to do battle with Mrs Moss.

She is waiting for me, like a spider sitting in her web. She's surrounded by the injured and the fallen. Craig from Year Four is sitting next to her, bent double and suffering audibly. I have every sympathy for him. Jordan Bates kicked me in the same spot last year and it still hurt a week later! I didn't know such pain was possible!

Mrs Moss has spotted me. 'Right, what have you got to say for yourself?'

I pause. I ponder. 'Let me see, miss. What *have* I got to say for myself? How about *Zippedy-doo-da?* Or perhaps, *Fiddle-dee-dee?* Or maybe, *Ging-gang-gooly-gooly-gooly-gooly-whatsit, ging-gang-goo, ging-gang-goo?*'

She glares at me. 'Don't try to be funny with me, young man.'

'I wasn't *trying* to be funny, miss,' I say. 'I was *succeeding*!'

She holds her hand up towards me, as if stopping traffic. 'I'd hold it right there if I were you. You're already in enough trouble as it is. Craig here says . . .'

'. . . that I kicked him.'

Mrs Moss is taken aback.

I continue. 'If Craig took the trouble to wear his glasses, he would have seen that it wasn't me. It was Ryan Snelling.'

She looks disappointed and turns towards Craig. 'Is that true, Craig?'

A moan comes from somewhere in between Craig's legs. 'Might be, miss.'

'But why did you say *he* did it?' She points at me, but Craig isn't looking.

No answer. Just moans and groans.

'*I'll* tell you why, miss,' I volunteer. 'It's because he knows that if he tells on Snelling, he'll get kicked again, twice as hard.'

'Is that true, Craig?'

'Uuuuhhhhh . . .'

Mrs Moss turns to me. 'Right, I suppose you can go then.'

Oh. Fine.

No apology, then.

No, of course not.

How silly of me to expect it!

'And by the way,' she adds, 'your name's going in my book.'

'What for?' I protest. 'Craig just *told* you I didn't do it.'

'Yes, well, I don't like your attitude, and I don't like

your cheek.' She starts scribbling in her little yellow book.

I don't believe this! Where's justice when you need it?

Justice? They can't even spell it around here!

The day's not really going according to plan. No matter what I aim to do, there's always somebody else with different ideas ready to mess it up for me.

The next hour passes in a blur. Before I know it, it's time for the baseball trials – Part Two!

Mr Taylor chooses two sides, with me as one of the captains. The game is a carbon-copy of the game we played last time round. I hit three home-runs, one after the other, and nearly hit Mr Batty's car with the last one!

And then it comes to that moment when I'm standing at second base and Mr Taylor is pointing at me and shouting: 'Out!'

Instead of coming up with some smart-alec remark or arguing with him, I surprise myself by just accepting the decision and walking off. I figure it's about time I gave my motor-mouth a rest.

As I sit down with the other players who are already out, I get a few pats on the back. Somebody says: 'Hard luck, Artie, that was close.' Somebody else says: 'Nice batting, mate.'

And when the match finishes twenty minutes later, Mr Taylor comes over to me, tells me that he's impressed with my attitude as well as my ability, that I might have what it takes to be captain of the school team!

Woh!

I can't believe what a huge difference one little change in behaviour can make! One minute I'm dropped from the team; the next minute I'm the captain!

I feel like I'm floating on air as I bound up the school steps at half past three.

But I soon fall back down-to-earth with a thud!

'KING!'

Mr Griffiths's voice seems to echo off every wall on the building.

'Back here, NOW!'

Every person in Bettws must have heard him!

Back down the steps I trudge and sit in his pongy office while he writes a letter to my mum, presumably explaining why I'm on 'holiday' for the rest of the week. He takes ages writing it, putting his pen to his mouth while he carefully chooses each word. I'm sure he's doing it on purpose!

When he finally releases me, I decide to take a shortcut home across the school field, to avoid Jordan and his little gang, but I only get so far when I'm called back. I'm not allowed to go this way because it's 'too secluded and you never know what strange people might be lurking in the woods'.

Strange people??!! What about all the strange people in *this* place? And since when did Mr Griffiths care about *my* welfare?

I drag myself up the steps, knowing full well what's waiting for me at the top.

And here they are, right on cue – Jordan Bates and the Odd Squad!

Jordan is busy re-arranging the hedge.

'Well, well, look who it isn't!' he observes. 'It's Art-Attack!'

Thanks again, Mum, for my lovely name!

'You're just in time,' he continues. 'We need your help.'

'Do you?' I say. 'Well, that's tough, isn't it, because I'm not available for any window smashing.'

This is brave talk.

Wayne and Dean look dumbstruck – even more dumbstruck than they normally do.

Jordan abandons his hedge-decorating and stands face-to-face with me.

'Tough?' he frowns. '*Tough*?'

I try to squeeze past. 'Look, sorry, I'm in a rush. I haven't got time for this.'

All three of them take a startled step back. Quite funny to see.

'Blinking 'eck!' declares Wayne. 'He must be psychic.'

'Cor,' says Dean, 'I reckon he's an alien. I always thought he was weird. How did he know about smashing the window?'

'Shut up, you two,' says Jordan, impatiently. 'If you had half a brain between you, you'd be dangerous. Somebody give him a rock.'

A stone is jammed into my hand.

Jordan speaks again. 'Listen, King. I have no idea how you knew what we're going to do – I've always had my suspicions that you're not normal – but it's not important anyway. You've got the rock, and there's the window!'

He points down at Mr Griffiths's office.

'I know you're a good shot,' he says, encouragingly. 'You shouldn't have any trouble hitting that from here. Nobody's watching.'

I glance down the steps. I can just make out part of Mr Griffiths's back and the pretty graphs on his laptop.

All of a sudden, I'm feeling very tempted to do as I've been asked.

After all, what has Mr Griffiths ever done for me, apart from nag me, lecture me and tell me off?

And nobody *is* watching!

What have I got to lose anyway?

I'll be meeting Lyn in a few minutes. He'll give me the tape-recorder and I can go back in time again, if I want to! If anything goes wrong, I can always *re-rewind!!* Can't I?

I weigh the rock in my hand and then launch it, with all my might, towards Mr Griffiths's window.

I push Jordan out of the way and run!

Behind me, there's a loud smash.

Louder than I would have imagined!

I hear Wayne's panic-stricken voice shouting: 'Let's get out of here. Quick!'

I don't bother looking behind me. I'm outta there too!

Chapter 9

Consequences

Who would have thought it possible that I could cover the distance from the school to the park even more quickly than last time? And yet I do!

And it's not even as if anyone is chasing me! Jordan and his buddies have headed off in the opposite direction, obviously making as much distance as they can between themselves and the scene of the crime!

As I enter the park, I get this horrible sinking feeling that Lyn won't be there and I'll be stuck with the here-and-now that I've just created. And if anyone saw me throwing that rock, the police will soon be paying me a visit!

I really need that tape-recorder!

Please, old man, please be there! Please be there . . .

And there he is . . . sitting in the same place, dozing on the park-bench, his head resting on the jacket of his pin-striped suit, his hands resting on his cane.

Thank you, God!

I don't remember ever having felt so happy to see someone!

I walk over and plonk myself down on the bench next to him.

No reaction.

He sits perfectly still. Unnaturally still.

That's *all* I need! He's gone and *died* on me!

I'm just about to check whether he's breathing or not when he stirs from his slumbers.

He blinks a few times, yawns and stretches.

'Hello there, young fella,' he says. 'Had a good day in school, have you?'

'Actually, not bad at all, thanks.'

It hadn't been *all* great, of course, but there *had* been some great bits, like driving Mr Batty nuts, humiliating Callum Young, telling Clare and Rachel what I thought of them, having some fun with Mrs Moss . . .

Best of all, though, had been the baseball! Mr Taylor telling me how good I was!

'Splendid,' Lyn comments. He seems to be staring off into some far-distant time or place. Or galaxy, for all I know!

'Anyway,' I add, 'it was a *lot* more fun the *second* time around.'

'Second time around?' he says, looking alarmingly bemused. 'I'm not sure I get your meaning.'

'You *know*,' I explain, 'the tape-recorder.'

'The what?'

Uh-oh.

This *cannot* be happening.

'The tape-recorder?' I repeat. 'The one you gave me yesterday.'

Lyn scratches his closely-shaven head. 'I'm sorry, young fella. Have we met before?'

Have we met before? *Have we met before??!!*

What the heck is going on ? I'm in big trouble here.

I didn't think it was possible for my life to get any worse.

But it just has.

In the last seven hours I've done some things that I'm *already* regretting. I was intending to rewind some of them!

Do I *really* have to face the consequences of the stupid things I've said and done today?

There'll be tears from my mum when she finds out I'm off school for the rest of the week. I have to admit, I haven't provided her with a lot of good news over the last couple of years.

Mr Batty certainly won't let me get away with the way I've talked to him today. He'll have it in for me. I can definitely say goodbye to the Oakwood trip. Callum Young is going to want revenge, big-time. Probably Ryan Snelling too! And if anybody finds out that I'm the phantom window-smasher, then I may end up chucked out of school altogether!

Still, at least I've got three new buddies in Jordan, Wayne and Dean! Every cloud has a silver lining, eh!

Lyn pulls a packet of polos from his jacket-pocket and offers me one. 'I always find a polo helps on occasions like these,' he says.

I take the polo. 'Thanks. That'll help a *lot!*'

He offers his hand for me to shake. 'Pleased to make your acquaintance, lad. Lyn's the name . . .'

And then he winks at me. 'But you probably *know* that already.'

He's been playing games with me. I feel like punching him in the arm, but he's probably got arthritis or something. I would never have guessed that an OAP could have such a twisted sense of humour!

He smirks. 'Not interested in games then, are you? Somebody of *your* age? How sad.'

He's peering at me over the top of his glasses, still smirking. 'Listen, young fella, as we discussed before, we *all* have good days and bad days. I'm glad you had some fun today, but you didn't exactly do what I hoped. You had a second chance . . .'

'. . . and I blew it?'

'Yes, as you say, you well and truly *blew* it.'

'But *how* did I blow it? I had fun. Isn't that what life's supposed to be about? Having a good time?'

Lyn leans forward and turns in my direction, suddenly looks quite stern. 'Life may *well* be about having fun, but there's slightly *more* to it than that. Life is about getting things right, making the right choices; it's about treating other people the way that you'd like them to treat *you*; and it's about learning from your mistakes, becoming a *better* person.'

'Oh, is *that* all?' I say, sarcastically.

Lyn looks more than stern now. He looks angry. I've upset him.

'Look,' I defend myself, 'I don't think I had a particularly bad day. It's not as if I killed anybody or anything, is it?'

Lyn suddenly leans on his stick and stands up. He is tall, even though his back is bent. He stands right in front of me, partly covering me with his shadow.

And then he says, slowly and deliberately: 'Are you

prepared to live with the consequences of your actions today?'

I have a quick think about it. The worst thing I've done is smash a window.

'Yes,' I declare confidently.

Lyn takes a step nearer to me, enveloping me completely in the darkness of his shadow. He looks around, as if there might be spies listening in to our conversation.

'I think it's time you were made aware of a few things.'

'What things?'

'Well, perhaps you need to be more familiar with what is going on in *other* people's lives.'

'Eh?'

'Mr Batty, for example.'

'Mr Batty?' I have no idea where this is going.

'Yes. Mr Batty, whose wife is very ill. Mr Batty, who hasn't got much of a sense of humour. Mr Batty, who will go home tonight and shed a few tears because of the day he has just had, dealing with children who have far too much to say for themselves.'

I stare in total disbelief at the crazy old man in front of me. 'There's *no* way you can know all that about Mr Batty.'

'Hmmm,' ponders Lyn, 'just like there's *no* way that tape-recorders can make three-year-old girls fall *up* the stairs? And there's *no* way that pigs can fly?'

I suppose I shouldn't be at all surprised that a man who owns a time-travelling tape-recorder can also see into people's lives. And read their minds!

I'm not sure what he means by the pigs, though! Pigs can't fly. Can they?

'Something else,' Lyn continues. 'What if I told you that Callum Young couldn't help what he did in assembly today?'

'Couldn't help it! Come on! You've got to be joking!'

'Yes. Couldn't help it. He has parents who completely ignore and neglect him and he will do anything to get attention.'

This is crazy!

'Were you *in* assembly today, by any chance?' I ask, totally confounded.

Lyn sits back down next to me. 'Well, yes and no.'

'Yes and no?'

'That's right.'

'Is there anything else I should know?' I ask, my curiosity growing.

'As a matter of fact, there is. That girl you've been talking to recently . . .'

'Gwyneth.'

'Yes. Gwyneth. Lovely name. Would you be interested to know that, about five minutes ago, on the way home from school, she was . . . well . . . set upon by two bigger girls, called . . . um, let me see . . .'

'Rachel and Clare?'

It had to be them! Who else could it be?

'That's right. Not exactly delicate little flowers, are they?'

No they're not!

'Is she OK?'

Lyn closes his eyes, then opens them again. 'She'll be fine. Just shaken up.'

'But I don't understand. How is what *they* do *my* fault?' I ask, becoming quite frustrated.

Lyn leans forward on his stick. 'I didn't say it was *your* fault. But how would *you* like being called ugly, nasty and evil?'

It wouldn't bother me! Besides, they *are* ugly, nasty and evil!

'And then there's the little lad at lunchtime,' adds Lyn.

'Who? Gavin Price?'

'No, the young man who got kicked.'

'You mean Craig. I never touched him.'

'I'm aware of that, but, because Ryan Snelling is *now* taking the blame for the incident, he has decided to make Craig's life a misery for the rest of his junior school life.'

I shrug my shoulders. 'You can't pin *that* one on me. *I* didn't call him Ryan *Smelling*!'

'I know,' Lyn nods his head. 'I'm just trying to make you understand that every little decision you make in life has an impact on *other* people, sometimes more than you know. Every action you perform has consequences.'

He's getting deep and serious again.

I just want to know when he's going to give me the tape-recorder.

'And then there's Mr Griffiths, of course.'

'What about Mr Griffiths?' I ask nervously.

A siren interrupts us. An ambulance siren.

I suddenly have a sickening thought. I virtually jump off the bench. 'That's *not* for Mr Griffiths, is it?'

'Why? Are you interested? Or would you rather have another polo? You seem to have just bitten that one in half.'

'Is Mr Griffiths OK?'

'Well, I suppose so,' mumbles Lyn, 'apart from the fact that he has a splinter of glass in his left eye.'

'What!!?? But he had his back to the window!'

I look at Lyn but he just shrugs.

'Is Mr Griffiths all right?' I ask.

Lyn strains his eyes as if he's trying to see something. 'Can't tell.'

'But I thought you knew *every*thing.'

In fact, I'm starting to wonder if he's God or something – he knows so much!

Lyn stands up again. 'Don't be a fool, boy. Nobody knows *every*thing!'

I don't like being called *boy*.

He starts to walk away. No, *stride* away!

I can't believe this is happening to me.

Mr Griffiths, in an ambulance, heading for the hospital!

I've got some enormous consequences to deal with here!

Let's face it, I'm in trouble with a capital T!!

Where's the tape-recorder?

I shout after Lyn: 'Wait a minute. Aren't you going to help me?'

He shows no sign of stopping.

'Wait!' I can feel myself pleading. 'Come on! It was *you* who got me into this mess!'

I don't like the way I sound. I always seem to be blaming other people.

Lyn stops in his tracks. I run after him. He turns towards me, puts his hands together like he's praying and glares at me over the top of his glasses.

'I did warn you,' he says, 'to be careful what you wish for.'

'Look, I need another chance, please.'

I'm reduced to begging.

'I usually only give *one* chance,' he says. 'What makes *you* such a special case?'

I've got no answer for this. I can't come up with a single reason why I deserve a second chance.

I start to walk away.

But then I feel a hand on my shoulder. 'Listen, young fella, I know you think you've got it hard, what with your father going away, a mother who has to spend more time with your little sister than you, and some teachers who give you more-than-your-fair-share of attention . . .'

A nice way of putting it.

'. . . but you *do* seem to wallow a bit. It's almost as if you actually *enjoy* being miserable and angry all the time.'

'But I . . .'

'Look, there is absolutely *nothing* you can do to make your dad come back. And, by the way, it's not your mum's fault that he's gone – or yours either!'

This last remark really hits home.

I feel my eyes beginning to water.

Lyn abruptly turns on his heel and heads towards the invisible hole in the hedge.

'Hang on, hang on!' I yell after him, in desperation. 'What about the tape-recorder?'

He keeps right on walking this time. I can vaguely hear him muttering about ups and downs, highs and lows, and what sounds like Ying and Yang!

Before I know it, he's gone. Where to, I have no idea! Another dimension? Another planet?

I wipe my eyes dry.

Well, isn't this just brilliant? What am I supposed to do now? I'm excluded for four days, my mother's going to be devastated, my new 'girlfriend' has been attacked and probably blames me, I've lost all hope of the Oakwood trip, and, to top it all, my headmaster is in hospital and it's my fault.

I've ruined any chance of turning over a new leaf.

How can I turn over a new leaf when I've *destroyed the book*?

I turn around in anger and frustration and promptly trip over . . . a shopping-bag.

Chapter 10

Love and Kisses

I pick myself up off the floor and check out the bag.

The tape-recorder's inside, all right, but there's no wrapping-paper or label this time.

Did Lyn plan on giving it back to me all along?

Or is this a last-minute change-of-mind?

Who cares? I've got another chance. I may not deserve it; in fact I *know* I definitely *don't* deserve it, but I've got another chance!

Of course, there's nothing stopping me from hitting the 'rewind' button straight away! But I hesitate. Now is *not* the time to be making make rash judgments, to be rushing in like a bull at a gate. I don't imagine there'll be any more chances after this one! I need time to think carefully about how I'm going to get things right this time. Third time lucky and all that!

I take my 'time-machine' home and hide it in the shed behind the hose-pipe. I need to gather my thoughts and plan my perfect day.

'Where've you been, luv?' Mum calls out from the kitchen.

I decide not to bother with my *helping Mr Batty* story. Mum seemed to have a hard time believing that one, last time.

'Mr Griffiths wanted to see me about something.'

There's a pause in the potato-mashing. 'You're not in trouble, are you, Art?'

She doesn't know the half of it!

'No. Of course not.'

She blocks my way as I try to get through the kitchen. She grabs me by the neck of my jersey and plants a kiss on my forehead. 'I was worried about you. There are a lot of weird people out there. You should have phoned.'

'Sorry, Mum,' I say and return the kiss.

She is taken aback, I can see, and looks puzzled. She asks me if I'm OK.

'Never better,' I smile. 'I'll sit at the table, shall I? I expect tea's almost ready.'

I am being a very good boy!

She frowns at me. 'Are you sure you're all right? You look like the canary who swallowed the cat!'

I laugh. She's always getting things the wrong way round. 'I think you mean the cat who swallowed the canary. And I'm just dandy, thanks. I had a great day, that's all.'

Well, I'm *about* to have one, anyway!

'You'll have to tell me all about it then, won't you. We'll sit down together later on when Sali's gone to bed.'

I grab the tomato sauce from the cupboard before Sali has a chance to get rid of it all.

She is sitting on her two cushions, waiting for her food. I grab her two rosy cheeks and give her a kiss. This is not like me at all!

'Uuuuuughh!' she screams. 'Mu-um, Artie kissed me!'

My mum looks at me like I'm a recent visitor to the planet Earth!

'Artie?!'

'What? Can't I kiss my sister?'

Mum shakes her head.

During the meal, Sali manages to hit me with a few minor splats of sauce, but I make some kissy-kissy-faces at her and she soon stops. I think I've got her worried!

I remind Mum about her aerobics lesson.

'Ooooh, I forgot to say,' she says. 'You'll have to watch Sali for me.'

'No problemo.'

'You know what. You're a *doll*!' she says, giving me yet another kiss. I've never had so many!

The next hour flies by. I sit in my red-and-white room thinking about the choices I've got to make in the day that lies ahead of me. I'm like a director planning out the scenes of a film. I run each scene, frame by frame, in my head.

Before I know it, it's time for Mum to go.

She stands in the doorway. 'Now you promise not to take your eyes off her. I'll be back just after seven.'

'You can trust me, Mum.' And that's never been more true!

My cheek is hit with yet *another* kiss. Erosion will be taking place soon!

Off Mum toddles across the road. I quickly grab Sali

from behind the curtains and manage to make her sit still by threatening to kiss her again.

I've already hidden *Barbie and the Nutcracker* upstairs. There's no way I'm sitting through that again!

I kneel down in front of the telly, sifting through some videos.

'What do you want to watch, Sal?'

'Barbie! Barbie!'

No surprises there, then!

I make a 'thorough' search and then shrug my shoulders. 'Can't find it.'

I wait for an outburst but none occurs.

There's a sigh from behind me and then Sali appears by my side. She reaches out for the video-player and presses the 'eject' button. Out pops a video. I'll give you three guesses what it is!

When I hid the *Barbie* video under my bed earlier on, I obviously neglected to check whether the cassette was actually inside the case. I put an *empty* cassette-box under my bed! *Plonker!*

Sali pushes the tape back in the machine and settles herself comfortably on the sofa. Oh joy!

Serves myself right for lying to a three-year-old!

After ten minutes of pure agony watching Barbie pirouetting all over the place – under rainbows, over toadstools and through forests – I'm all Barbied out! I just want to go out to the shed and grab the tape-recorder.

I check on the toilet situation first.

'Sali, do you need the toilet?'

No answer. Trance-like state.

I stand between her and Barbie. 'Sali, do you need a wee?'

Her head jigs from side to side as she endeavours to see past me.

'NOOOOOO!!!!' she shrieks like a banshee. 'Get out of my WAAAAYYYY!'

Right! I grab this window of opportunity and head out through the kitchen. The shed-door is open. I don't remember leaving it open! I scoot inside and . . .

It isn't there!!!

I rummage around, searching in every nook and cranny. I definitely left it behind the hose-pipe! I feel around every inch of the floor, giving myself a splinter in the process.

Where could it have gone? I'm having trouble breathing. I think it's called a panic attack.

I can't hang about here. I'm supposed to be watching Sali.

What am I going to do?

And then, scooting back through the kitchen, I spot it, sitting there as bold as brass on the kitchen counter. There's a piece of paper next to it with my mum's writing on it:

Art, Do you know who this belongs to? Found it in the shed. Love, Mum.

Strange. Why didn't she say anything before she went?

Still, who cares?

I pick it up tenderly and hold it like a baby. I hug it. I kiss it.

My preciousss!

All of a sudden, I become aware that the TV has gone awfully quiet. Barbie and her nutcracker usually make more noise than that!

I head for the living-room.

'Everything all right, Sal . . ?'

The TV image has frozen Barbie in mid-prance!

Sali is nowhere to be seen!

Why does nothing ever go according to plan?

There's a loud thud from upstairs. My heart tries to escape through my ribs! Sali has obviously just bounded onto the top stair! I thought she said she didn't need the toilet!

One second from now, she is going to come falling down the stairs like a rag doll. I'll never get there in time!

Then I remember I don't have to! *Time* is at my beck and call!

I press down on the 'rewind' button and close my eyes.

Third time lucky!

Chapter 11

Last Chance

'Arrtttiieeeeee!!! Wake up!!! You're going to be late again!!!'

I don't think so.

Not *this* time!

I'm a man on a mission. I *am* going to get to school on time. I *am* going to get to school on time. I *am* . . .

I brush my teeth, comb my hair and grab my uniform. I'm still wrestling with it as I hit the top stair, which probably explains why I lose my footing and fall. I literally bounce down the stairs, well, halfway down at least. This may look funny to spectators (thank goodness there aren't any!) but it certainly doesn't feel funny!

Mum appears behind me on the landing.

I can't move. I let out a moan.

What a brilliant start! What did Lyn say about ups and downs?

Mum comes running down after me. If she goes and falls now, that'll be three members of the same family in one day! That's got to be good enough to get us in the Guinness Book of Records!

'Are you all right?' she says anxiously, sitting down next to me.

Do I *look* all right?

I straighten up a bit, move my limbs, one by one, to see if they still work properly.

'I think I am.'

'What were you playing at? You came out of your room like a supercharged rocket!'

'Nothing,' I groan. 'I just thought it might be nice *not* to be late for a change, that's all.'

A look of guilt passes over my mother's face. 'Oh. It's probably *my* fault. I ought to get you up earlier, I know. It's just that I know how much you like your sleep.'

My eyes start to fill up. 'Yeah, but I keep getting in trouble for being late.'

'Oh, I'm sorry, luv,' she says, putting her arm around my shoulder.

'Oooooww!' *Not* the best moment to give me a hug! 'Well, if I didn't break any bones before, I have now!'

'Cheeky!' Mum smiles and hugs me again, even harder.

'Oooyyyy!'

She helps me up, slowly. 'I think you ought to stay home for a bit, Art, just to make sure you're all right.'

I have to be honest, it's tempting. But I do actually *want* to go to school, to put things right.

'I'm OK, Mum, honestly,' I reassure her.

'Well I don't know. As long as you're sure. But you'd better get your skates on if you're not going to be late.'

What? Holy mackerel!

The fates are conspiring against me yet again!

'Gotta go, Mum!'

I hurry down the remaining few steps and head out the front door.

A few strides into my journey, I realize that running is out of the question. Even walking is difficult. I'm starting to ache all over.

I look at my watch. It's a quarter to nine. I can still get there on time if I keep up a good steady pace. Keep walking!

On I plod, picking up some funny looks along the way. I could so easily win a silly-walk competition right now.

I've got two minutes to spare as I reach the school gates. I struggle down the steps and hobble around the school buildings to the yard.

It's quiet.

Very quiet.

No wonder! Nobody's there! The yard is empty.

I check my watch again; it's one minute to nine!

I glance to my left through my classroom windows. Rhys Williams's ugly mug is grinning back at me. They're *all* in there! The whistle must have gone already. I don't understand, unless my watch is wrong.

Rhys is now talking to Mr Batty and pointing at me.

Here we go again!

I make my way inside the building. The classroom door lies open. It's deathly silent. If a mouse had chosen this moment to burp, the whole class would have heard it.

I take a deep breath and walk in.

'HURRRRRAAAYYYYYY!!!!!'

I nearly have a heart attack.

The classroom erupts with cheers and applause.

I'm frozen. My eyes are the only part of me to move, darting from side-to-side. I'm wondering what the heck's going on? Have I rewound a day or been transported to another dimension?

The eruption dies down.

I walk over to Mr Batty's desk. He doesn't look up straight away.

'Yes?' he eventually says.

'Er . . . I'm sorry I'm late, sir, only I . . .'

'Yes, well, *that's* the thing, isn't it.'

'Eh?'

'You're *not* late.'

I look around, then scratch my head. 'But . . .'

'Yes, I know it must *look* like you're late, but Mrs Lewis was on duty and her watch was five minutes fast, so when she blew her whistle it was actually only five to nine. So, that means . . . you are actually *on* time, which explains the applause . . . and the sticker I'm about to give you.'

He breaks into a semi-smile and places the sticker on my chest. It's got a picture of a cartoon tiger on it, and it says 'GRRREAT'. I'm not sure if it's a genuine sticker or a 'sarcastic' sticker. It feels genuine.

'Well done,' he says. 'Nice to see you in on time. Try and keep it up.'

'Yes, sir.'

I feel like I'm ten-foot tall as I walk over to my seat. Gwyneth smiles at me.

My behaviour over the next hour is impeccable:

I actually put my hand up when I know the answer to some questions instead of shouting out the first thing that comes into my head like I normally do; *and* I manage to finish some work on time; *and* it's neat with hardly any spelling mistakes; *and* I underline the date and title – all the things that keep Mr Batty a happy chappy.

He asks me if I'm feeling all right and starts to sound like my mother.

Assembly-time arrives and, right on schedule, Callum plays his one-note symphony.

The prayer comes to a sudden halt.

Everyone looks towards us.

I do not go red. I sit there as cool as a cucumber. Callum and I are a *pair* of cool cucumbers.

'Was that you, Callum Young?' Mr Griffiths enquires.

'No, sir.' Cool as cool can be.

Mr Griffiths pauses for a moment . . . and then continues with the prayer as if nothing has happened.

And nothing more does happen. I finally make it *all* the way through assembly without attracting Mr Griffiths's attention and make it back to class without a visit to the headmaster's office.

I get more playtime too! Bonus!

Out on the field, Gwyneth is walking arm-in-arm with Rachel and Clare. I catch up with them, but they make no sign of stopping, so I get in front of them and walk backwards.

'*My, my,*' comments Clare, 'who's being a good little boy today, then?'

'What happened?' asks Rachel. 'Did you get out of bed on the *right* side today, for a change?'

I obviously can't win with these two. Being good earns me no more respect than being bad.

'I'm just trying to turn over a new leaf,' I explain.

'Once a creep, always a creep,' comments Clare.

'Anyway,' Rachel smiles, 'd'ya mind? You're in the way?'

'Yeah, shove off, creep!'

Gwyneth hasn't said a thing. She's stuck between the two of them.

What to do now?

On the yard behind them, there's a football match going on. Luke Davies is captaining one of the teams and Christopher Watkins the other. Both Luke and Chris are tall, blonde, strong and, I suppose you would say, good-looking. Girls are always dumping their boyfriends so that they can go out with one of these two.

'Hey, girls!' I say. 'Bet you don't know what Chris and Luke were saying about you earlier on.'

The threesome comes to a halt.

'Get stuffed, King!'

Charming.

'Well, if you don't want to know . . .' I say, walking away.

I travel about six paces when Rachel's voice behind me asks: 'So, what did they say . . . *not* that we believe you or anything?'

I turn around. 'They said they want to meet you and Clare at the top of the steps straight after school.'

'What for?'

'I have no idea.'

'Why would they tell *you* to tell us?'

'I have no idea.'

'Do you know *anything* about anything, King?'

'I have no idea.'

Sometimes I'm so funny I make myself laugh.

Clare stares at me suspiciously. 'How do we know you're not lying, you rat-bag?'

'Go and ask them yourselves.'

They take the bait. They ask Gwyneth to go with them, but she says she's too embarrassed, so off the two of them head for the yard.

There's an awkward silence, while Gwyneth and I try to think of something to say to each other. 'So,' she says, 'were you telling the truth, then?'

Mrs Lewis blows the whistle before I can give her an answer. Rachel and Clare haven't even got as far as the yard. The footballers pick up their ball and start lining up.

Mission accomplished.

Gwyneth shouldn't be faced with any problems after school this evening. Rachel and Clare will be too busy waiting around for their new boyfriends!

Chapter 12

Justice for All

Back in class, it's science revision again. We seem to have had an awful lot this week!

'Only six weeks to go till those lovely end-of-year tests!' declares Mr Batty – again!

'Ten pence, sir.'

'Thank you, Rhys. What would I do without you?'

'Ah yes, I nearly forgot,' continues Mr Batty. 'Before we start, I need to collect this week's homework.'

And off he wanders around the classroom collecting in pieces of paper.

It's not too long before he's standing in front of me.

'Well?' he enquires.

There's not much I can do. What can I say? I don't know why I didn't do the stupid homework. I've had three chances. I must be a moron or something!

'Er . . . I haven't . . . done it . . . sir.'

Mr Batty looks at me as if I've lost my marbles. 'Don't be daft,' he says. 'What's this, then?' He is holding a piece of paper which he has just picked up from the corner of my desk – a piece of paper which wasn't there five seconds ago. It is completely blank.

Mr Batty seems to be scanning it but I can't think why – there's nothing on it! Then, to my amazement, he comments that it looks good and moves on.

Lyn's been up to something!

One thing is certain: I'll be making an effort to get my homework done on time from now on. I might as well get in training for the High School. They get homework every night over there!

When the bell rings, I stay sitting at my desk for a few extra seconds, with a smile so big it nearly falls off my face. This morning has been a success. I feel like I've finally got round an obstacle course after failing it repeatedly.

Things go really well with Gwyneth at lunchtime. We have a whole bunch of things to talk about and loads of things in common.

I am ready for little Gavin Price and, at the precise moment that he taps me on the shoulder, I spin towards him, pretend to snap at his hand with my teeth, then roar like a rabid animal. 'RAAAARGGHHH!'

Gwyneth finds this funny, but Gavin doesn't. Back-pedalling, and from a safe distance, he yells at me: 'Mrs Moss wants to see you!'

'What do you think that's about?' Gwyneth asks.

'She probably wants to give me a medal,' I joke. 'I won't be a minute.'

As I take the long walk inside, I decide to play this scene straight. My tongue has got me into a lot of trouble lately.

It's starting to feel really peculiar, meeting the same situations over and over again. Talk about *déjà vu*!

Mrs Moss has the welcome mat out ready for me. 'At last! And what do you have to say for yourself?'

'Nothing, miss' I reply, doing my best to be humble.

'Nothing? How typical! Craig here gets kicked, and what do you have to say for yourself? Nothing.'

'*I* didn't do it, miss.'

She pulls a weird face. If she could see what she looks like, she wouldn't pull it.

'Look, Craig says you did.'

Oh, in that case, it must be true then!

'Look, miss . . .' I try to explain.

'Don't you *look* me! Craig doesn't tell lies. If he says you did it, you did it!'

This is starting to look more and more like a no-win situation.

But just when I start thinking all is lost, who should come to the rescue but Rhys Williams. But he's not on his own. He's being dragged in by Luke Davies and Christopher Watkins. His legs no longer seem to be working properly.

Mrs Moss gets quickly to her feet. 'Whatever's the matter?'

'Ryan Snelling kicked him, miss!' says Christopher.

'Oh,' Mrs Moss says, taken aback, 'you'd better bring him over here.' Rhys is duly brought over and eased into the chair next to Craig. He immediately takes up the same position as Craig – head between the legs.

'Did you see it happen?' Mrs Moss asks them.

'Yeah, miss,' says Luke. 'And that's the *second* person he's kicked in the last ten minutes. Somebody needs to sort him out!'

'Oh,' she says. 'Who *else*?'

Glaringly obvious, isn't it?

They point at Craig.

'Oh,' Mrs Moss says again. Her vocabulary seems to be getting shorter by the minute.

'Do you know *why* he kicked Craig?' she asks.

'Because Craig called him Ryan *Smelling*, instead of Snelling. By accident, we think.'

'Oh. And why did he kick *Rhys*?'

'Dunno, miss. Probably just for being Rhys. He *is* a pain.'

'Oh, right then. Would you please do me a favour, boys? Would you please go and get Mr Purvis?'

Mr Purvis is our deputy head. Getting him is a wise move. There is no way that Ryan Snelling is going to come quietly. Mr Purvis is definitely the right man for the job!

Luke and Chris go and fetch him.

I'm left standing. Mrs Moss is staring into space.

'Can I go then, miss?' I ask.

She wakes up from her trance. 'Uh . . . yes . . . sorry.'

I turn around and head outside. It's not until I've travelled a few steps that it hits me – Mrs Moss has just apologized. To *me*!

J-U-S-T-I-C-E. They *can* spell it around here, after all!

I'm shocked by the way people are treating me, just because I'm acting a little differently. I'm being treated like I'm not me any more!

Unbelievably, the baseball trials go even better than last time. I manage to avoid getting out by not making that reckless dash to second base. I score even more home-runs!

After the session, Mr Taylor tells me that my performance is the best he has ever seen by a boy of my age and he has no choice but to make me captain of the school team.

Cool!

At three thirty I am positively flying up the school steps! This may well be the best day I have ever had ...

'KING!!!' Mr Griffiths's voice booms up from behind me. I've obviously counted my chickens too early. 'Back here!'

Shoulders hunched, my elation gone in an instant, I make my way back down the steps.

What now?

I am beckoned into the headmaster's fragrant office. 'Sit yourself down,' he says.

I have a quick mental run-through of today. What could I have possibly done wrong *this* time?

'Well, King,' he begins, 'I think you've surprised us all today. I just wanted to say that, if this is the new you, I'm very impressed. And Mr Batty, Mr Taylor and Mrs Moss have all had good things to say about you today. Well done. I'll be expecting you to keep it up.'

He holds out his hand for me to shake. He has a very strong grip and nearly breaks my wrist. Probably revenge for being a pain for all these years!

Then he gives me this really snazzy certificate, which has been laminated. It says: WELL DONE – YOU'VE HAD A PERFECT DAY!

It's been signed by Mr Griffiths and Mr Batty. My mum is going to be well chuffed with this!

I bound right back up the steps, but, in my excitement, forget who's waiting at the top: Dracula, Frankenstein and the Mummy!

'Well, well! Look who it isn't! It's Art-Attack!'

It doesn't sound any funnier the third time of hearing it!

And then I notice, about ten metres further along the pavement, Rachel and Clare. Of course! They're waiting for their 'dates'! Luke and Chris have no idea that they're supposed to be outside the school right now. They're probably already home, having tea.

I give Rachel and Clare the thumbs-up sign. They turn the other way in disgust!

Jordan is busily destroying the hedge with his right foot. 'Just the person we were looking for,' he says.

I decide to counter-attack. 'Actually, it's funny you should say that, because *I* was looking for *you*! Well, not *you* exactly, but your two mates here.' I indicate Wayne and Dean.

'What are you on about?' he says, obviously taken off-guard for a second.

'Look,' I say, pointing at Rachel and Clare. 'You see those two over there? I expect you've seen them hanging about for the last ten minutes.'

'Yeah, so?'

'Well, they're a bit shy, but I know for a fact that they fancy Wayne and Dean. They're always talking about them in school.'

Jordan pulls a couldn't-care-less face, but the eyes of the other two light up like they've won the lottery or something. Like me, they've probably never had proper girlfriends. Rachel and Clare are not exactly super-stars but they're not she-monsters either! Wayne steps forward and actually puts his arm around me. 'Thanks for the info, mate,' he says. 'You're a pal.'

'Yeah,' adds Dean, giving me a friendly punch on the arm. 'Nice one.'

Jordan is getting visibly angry.

Wayne whispers something in Dean's ear. They both snigger and then set off towards the lucky girls.

Jordan looks like he's just been hit by a truck!

I take advantage of this and quietly slip away.

I'm tempted to comment: 'It's been *smashing* talking to you,' but think better of it!

I can't wait to tell Lyn about the day I've had. But then, going by what's happened so far, he probably already *knows*.

Before I turn the corner into Monnow Way, I take one last backward glance towards the school. I make eye-contact with Rachel. She makes a very unladylike gesture towards me. She probably wants to run after me and kill me, but she and Clare can't move at the moment because they're being hemmed in by these two affectionate pit bulls! It's so refreshing to see somebody else trapped for a change!

Chapter 13

A New Beginning

Lyn is exactly where he's supposed to be, enjoying his afternoon nap.

I hurl myself down on the bench with such force that he has no choice but to wake up.

He leaps up, amazingly agile for such an old man, shouting: 'The sword! The sword! Get the sword!' Then he twirls around, as if checking for enemies. Weird!

He looks down at me and then shakes the sleep out of his head. 'Hello there, young fella,' he says. 'Had a good day in school, have you?'

I pause. 'Actually, I've had more than a good day. I've had a practically perfect day.'

I must look pretty smug. I feel pretty smug.

'Ah yes,' he says, staring into the distance, 'some days are like that. Have a polo to celebrate.'

I take the offered polo and, while I suck it, tell Lyn all about my perfect day: about my sticker from Mr Batty and my certificate from Mr Griffiths; about me and Gwyneth; about being chosen as captain of the school baseball team. I tell him about how great it was to see justice being done and the right people being punished for their wrongdoings. Oh, and I tell him about my mysterious homework!

'That's rather odd,' he comments, without even the trace of a give-away smile.

Odd??!! He's not kidding, it's odd!

And what about little sisters falling down stairs and then falling back up them? What about a bed that shoots through walls and ceilings and flies along streets as if it's a hovercraft? What about tape-recorders with magical powers? What about old men who disappear through holes that are not even there?

Odd, he says! That's the understatement of the year!

He pats me on the knee. 'I'm so glad it all went well, Artie,' he says. It feels like he's my long-lost grandfather or something.

I suck my polo contentedly.

'Of course,' he continues, 'you *do* realize that the tape-recorder will now be staying with me.' He then reaches out in front of him and pulls the tape-recorder from out of thin air, then rests it on his lap!

I am dumbfounded. 'How did you do that?'

'Ah, that would be telling, wouldn't it? Anyway, as I was saying, this was meant to be a *once* in a life-time gift. You don't know how lucky you are to have had it twice! Most irregular!'

I nod. 'I understand. And thanks.'

Lyn looks surprised. 'You know, you're not the boy you were. I'm pleased you've learned something. That's what life is for, isn't it? Learning from our experiences.'

He stands up and faces me, resting both hands on the gold handle of his walking-stick. I'd never noticed before, but the gold part of the stick is carved in the shape of an owl. Its eyes are made of some shiny red stones, like rubies. They're staring at me right now.

Lyn rests his stick up against the bench and holds his hand out for me to shake. I stand up and offer my hand, which he immediately encloses in *both* of his. The strangest feeling shoots through my body, like electricity. It's just like I've plugged myself into a powerful generator and suddenly been sent a surge of energy. And Lyn's eyes stare into mine. No, not just *into*. It's almost as if he is seeing right inside me, reading my innermost thoughts and feelings.

He lets go and I nearly fall over. My legs feel like jelly.

Lyn shows no sign that something weird just happened. 'Now don't forget, lad,' he says. 'Not every day is going to be like today. Your life, like everybody else's life, is going to be one big rollercoaster of ups and downs and twists and turns.'

'I know.'

'I know you know.'

I'm tempted to say: 'I know you know I know,' but stop myself.

'And don't forget,' he continues, 'and this is *more* important. You don't have to just sit there and *accept* the downs. You can change the downs to ups, or at least stop them going into free-fall! What I'm saying is, if you make enough of the right decisions, you can have a ride with more ups than downs.'

He pats me on the shoulder. 'Anyway,' he smiles, 'you'll only be getting *one* life. You won't be able to rewind it and start again, that's for sure! My advice is, hold on tight and enjoy the ride!'

He picks up his stick and leads me over towards his 'hole' in the hedge. Of course, there *isn't* any hole.

'Will I be seeing you again?' I ask. I've grown quite attached to him.

'Well,' he ponders, 'it's not beyond the realms of possibility.'

'Am I allowed to know where you're from?' I don't know why I hadn't thought to ask him this before, especially with all this weird stuff going on. He can't be from anywhere normal, that's for sure!

He smiles and shakes his head. 'Not from these parts,' he says. Mysterious to the end!

'I gathered that.'

'Well that's all you need to know, then.'

He shakes my hand again, this time without any electrical effects.

'Well, Arthur,' he exclaims, 'I wish you good fortune in all your endeavours!'

Arthur?

'Please don't call me Arthur. My friends call me Art or Artie.'

His blue eyes crinkle up into a mysterious smile. Something is about to happen. I can feel it. My body starts to tingle. My hair is standing on end. This is spooky.

The wind suddenly picks up. I watch as some stray pieces of litter a few feet away from us are picked up in a sort of mini-tornado!

And then, from out of nowhere, butterflies appear. Hundreds of them. Silver butterflies. Every single one of them silver. They flutter and spiral around Lyn in a magical dance. I swear his feet leave the ground for a moment!

'And *my* friends call me MERLYN!' he declares, stretching his arms towards the heavens. 'Merlyn the Magical! Merlyn the Mysterious! Merlyn the Magnificent!'

What? What's happening here? Merlyn?

He actually *is* off the ground! Is anybody else seeing this?

He twirls around three times in a silver blur and, by the time he's stopped spinning, he looks exactly like Merlyn's supposed to look, with long white hair and pointy hat. And he truly does look magical, mysterious and magnificent!

My gob-smacked mouth probably resembles an open drawbridge.

'Oh,' he adds, with a knowing smile, 'and I forget to mention Merlyn the Modest.'

Lyn reaches across and closes my mouth for me. 'You'll stay like that if you're not careful,' he laughs.

'You mean,' I say, with great hesitation, 'you're the Merlyn who helped King Arthur?'

'As far as I know,' he frowns, 'there's only *one* Merlyn. It's not every Tom, Dick or Harry who can make time go backwards, y'know.'

He strides forward towards the hedge.

'But,' I struggle to express myself, 'how can a *man* do all the things that you can do?'

'Whoever said that I was a man?'

'I just assumed . . .'

'Never assume anything.'

'Well, if you're not a man, then what are you?'

He puts a finger to his nose and taps it. 'Ah, that would be telling.'

And then he's off towards the hedge again.

'Wait! Why would Merlyn want to help me? I'm just a boy who lives in Bettws with his mum and little sister. I'm just an insignificant little speck in the universe.'

He stops once again. He seems to be smiling and frowning at the same time, if that's possible. He comes right up to me, puts both hands on my shoulders and looks me right in the eye.

'You are *not* an insignificant little speck, and if I catch you saying or thinking that, I'll be back to see you and there'll be serious consequences. *No* human being is insignificant. Every one of those people out there, in Bettws or Wales or wherever, contributes something to the sum of human experience.'

The *what*?

'Oh.'

'You may well say, *Oh*.'

'But King Arthur was important.'

'You seem to forget. He was a skinny little boy once.'

Skinny little boy? Who's *he* calling a skinny little boy?

And then I come to my senses. *Wart* and the *Sword in the Stone* and all that! It's just a Disney film, isn't it? And King Arthur's just a legend. He may not even have been real!

Lyn looks me right in the eye. 'Don't even say it!' He raises his voice. 'Not real, indeed! What piffle!'

Perhaps he *was* real, then! Who am I to argue with a time-travelling wizard?

'I still don't understand why you picked me to help. Why not some other boy?'

Lyn, or should I say Merlyn, raises his eyes skywards in disgust. 'Tut-tut, use your brain for once, lad. Perhaps I know something that you don't. Perhaps the 'rewind' button is not the only button that I play around with!'

I ponder for a minute. 'You mean you've seen my future?'

He taps the bridge of his nose with his finger again. Annoying.

I'm completely befuddled. 'You don't mean that I'm going to be a king, do you?'

Merlyn bursts out laughing, nearly losing his hat. 'That would be something, wouldn't it, with a surname like yours! No, I think I can safely say that you *won't* become a king. No. Your achievement will surpass that of kings.'

Cool.

What could it all mean?

'And, furthermore,' he adds, 'you are going to need every ounce of confidence and self-belief if you are to succeed.'

I'm feeling more confident, if a little confused, already.

'And now,' Merlyn declares, 'I really must be going. Time waits for no man. Strange expression, that.'

He heads hedgewards yet again.

'I hope I see you again,' I call after him. This must sound a bit pathetic.

He stands up tall, as if taking a deep breath. 'I'LL BE BACK . . . SOME DAY!'

One second he's there; the next second he's gone. Not even a puff of magical smoke!

I stay staring at the hedge for a good ten minutes. Anybody walking past might think I'm having a funny turn or something!

I'm more than a little confused! I'm not at all sure whether recent events have been real or just a dream.

Things like this just *don't* happen!

And they certainly don't happen to people like me!

But something *must* have happened because I feel different! I don't feel so sorry for myself anymore. I feel like a new person.

I'm woken from my daydreaming by a huge magpie, which skims the top of my head and lands, squawking, on the hedge in front of me.

And then the same thing happens again!

Two of them!

One for sorrow, two for joy!

Whoop-eeee-doooo!

Things are looking up already.

Let the rollercoaster begin! I'm strapped in and ready for the ride of my life!